**Unable to re⬛⬛⬛⬛⬛⬛⬛⬛⬛⬛⬛⬛oft
kiss to the t⬛⬛⬛⬛⬛⬛⬛⬛
danced.**

"I spent the better part of the evening watching that cowboy follow you all over the damn field," he said.

She lifted her head, her brows drawing down. "Who? This is a ranch, Dominic. There's nothing but cowboys out here."

Laughter escaped him. "Nevertheless, I noticed one in particular that took a shine to you."

"I hope so," she returned softly.

His chest stilled on a deep breath. Those big, beautiful blues were on him again. Easing right through his skin, deep inside. They gazed up at him, soft and undemanding. Adoring, almost. So different from any other woman's.

A heavy weight unfolded in his gut and seeped into his veins. Who did she see? Dom, the champion bull rider full of good times? Or Dominic, the sometimes dependable guy who came through in a pinch?

And, more daunting still, could he live up to either?

Dear Reader,

I was born and raised in a small Southern town with three traffic lights, cows on every corner and sweet tea flowing out of every faucet. It's one of those rare places where you'll never meet a stranger and will always have a friend. A place I, and many others, proudly call home.

An analysis by the *New York Times* identified the county in which I reside as one of the top ten hardest places to live in America. The finding was surprising and, then again, not so surprising. We have more than our fair share of poverty and bad luck. But we also have wealth beyond measure. A wealth that resides in the beauty of the people. The same people who smiled, shook their heads and carried on with business as usual after hearing the news.

In *Twins for the Bull Rider*, Cissy Henley struggles to raise orphaned nephews. She has a meager amount of money and even less support. What she does have is grit, determination and a difficult decision to make. Cissy discovers what's most important in life is something money can never buy. And something that, most of the time, arrives when you least expect it.

Thank you for reading Cissy's story. I hope you feel at home on Raintree Ranch and visit again soon.

April Arrington

TWINS FOR
THE BULL RIDER

APRIL ARRINGTON

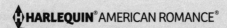HARLEQUIN® AMERICAN ROMANCE®

Recycling programs
for this product may
not exist in your area.

ISBN-13: 978-0-373-75618-6

Twins for the Bull Rider

Copyright © 2016 by April Standard

All rights reserved. Except for use in any review, the reproduction or utilization of this work in whole or in part in any form by any electronic, mechanical or other means, now known or hereinafter invented, including xerography, photocopying and recording, or in any information storage or retrieval system, is forbidden without the written permission of the publisher, Harlequin Enterprises Limited, 225 Duncan Mill Road, Don Mills, Ontario M3B 3K9, Canada.

This is a work of fiction. Names, characters, places and incidents are either the product of the author's imagination or are used fictitiously, and any resemblance to actual persons, living or dead, business establishments, events or locales is entirely coincidental.

This edition published by arrangement with Harlequin Books S.A.

For questions and comments about the quality of this book, please contact us at CustomerService@Harlequin.com.

® and TM are trademarks of Harlequin Enterprises Limited or its corporate affiliates. Trademarks indicated with ® are registered in the United States Patent and Trademark Office, the Canadian Intellectual Property Office and in other countries.

Printed in U.S.A.

www.Harlequin.com

April Arrington grew up in a small Southern town and developed a love for movies and books at an early age. Emotionally moving stories have always held a special place in her heart. During the day, she enjoys sharing classic literature and popular fiction with students. At night, she spends her time writing stories of her own. April enjoys collecting pottery and soaking up the Georgia sun on her front porch. You can follow her on Twitter, @april_arrington.

Dedicated to:

Aunt Joanie for getting me through rough times...
because that's just what great aunties do.

Dad. There's not a greater man walking the earth.

Billie Ann for all of your patient support.

Laura Barth and Kathleen Scheibling for giving a
small-town girl a shot at a big dream.

And...

Mama. I still miss you. Every day.

Chapter One

Trailer trash.

Cissy Henley cringed. She'd learned early on that living in a trailer had little to do with the label. Only poverty and desperation were prerequisites. And the foul-smelling man hovering behind her in the Peachy Keen Diner thought that was exactly what she was.

"Anybody home, baby?" He laughed. "I said, you reserving the place for me?"

Cissy straightened her shoulders and maintained her stance facing the restroom door. The flimsy sticker proclaiming MEN had a gash through the middle and sagged at the corners. She kept a firm eye on the faded wood, reminding herself that no one had entered it during the past few minutes. And she would ensure it remained that way.

"No," she said. "It's out of service for the moment."

"Yeah?" His croon dropped a notch, his hot breath hitting the back of her neck. "Well, whatcha say I hang with you till it's back in service?"

Cissy sighed. *Chauvinistic redneck.* Harassing a woman was probably the highlight of his Saturday night. He deserved a swift kick in the shins. Unfortunately, she couldn't afford to lose her temper.

Ignore him. He'll go away.

A stained T-shirt and hairy arms obstructed her vision. The man wedged himself between her and the door, flashing a smile that was all dingy teeth. He rubbed a lanky hand over the grizzled stubble of his chin.

"Not right for a lady like yourself to be all alone this late at night." The words slurred. He ran his bleary eyes over her face and down her chest, leaning back to survey her legs.

Trailer trash. Cheap. Easy. Her lip curled. She knew the words were flashing in his head.

Cissy ran her eyes over him, taking stock of his scrawny build and unstable frame. His hands trembled. Probably from too much liquor and too hard living. Harmless fool. But a fool nonetheless.

"I'm not alone." She elbowed her way to the other side of him and refocused on the bathroom door.

"No, not anymore." He shoved his face in front of hers. Delight pooled in his eyes. He licked his lips and leaned forward.

"I wasn't alone before you joined me," Cissy bit out. "Now, I suggest you take your ass on."

His smile faded. It took a moment for his unfocused gaze to register the soft words as a rejection. He blinked hard. "What's that?"

The bathroom door banged open. Two blond boys tumbled out, shoving at one another before barreling into them.

"Aunt Cissy, they ain't got no paper towels in there," Kayden, her six-year-old nephew, declared, dragging his palms over the other boy's shirt. Frowning, he looked the drunk at her side over from head to toe. "Who's he?"

Cissy quickly gathered the boys against her legs, unable to contain the grin that spread across her face. She lifted an eyebrow at the man's confusion.

His head swiveled, taking in the boys, then her and back again. It was clear rambunctious twin boys were not part of his agenda. He moved around them, limbs wobbling.

"You bothering my aunt Cissy?" Kayden clenched his fists and pulled against her hold, attempting to follow the man's stumbling steps into the bathroom.

"N-no, not at all," he stammered, easing away with an uncomfortable laugh. "Just making polite conversation is all." He nodded. "Was nice meetin' you."

"You, too," she called out with a saccharine smile.

"I'm starving." Jayden, the eldest twin, disentangled from her clutch and clamored up into a nearby booth.

Kayden tore away and settled beside his brother. They bent over a menu, leaning into each other.

Cissy frowned and thumbed through the bills at the edge of her pocket to calculate for the third time. *Seventeen dollars and sixty-two cents.* Unfortunately, her count had been correct the first time and remained so ever since. She slipped the bills back into her shorts, making sure all the coins were settled underneath, then plopped into the booth across from the boys.

"Aunt Cissy, they have triple-decker cheeseburgers." Kayden shoved a greasy menu in her face. His eyes sparkled as he pointed to the colorful close-up of a burger meal.

Mmm. Her mouth watered. She smashed it shut so she wouldn't drool on the table.

Seventeen dollars and sixty-two cents. She had to stretch that as far as it would go.

"And onion rings." Jayden bounced in his seat. He scooted to his brother's ear and shielded a conspiratorial whisper behind his hand.

Snatching up the mug in front of her, she forced a mouthful of coffee past the lump in her throat and winced as the bitter brew seized her taste buds. Her stomach churned and rumbled. She rubbed a hand over her belly. Even the leftover gummy bears from twelve hours ago would be a blessing right about now.

"They got hot-fudge sundaes," the boys sang in unison. "With whipped cream," they taunted.

A groan emerged as she imagined a cool dollop of sweet cream melting on her tongue. *Seventeen dollars and sixty-two cents!* a voice screamed inside her head.

"That's they *have* hot-fudge sundaes," she corrected. She held out a hand, unable to still the tremor running through it. "Boys, hand me the menu, please."

They grumbled but passed it over. She located the items they requested and forced her fingers to trail across the sticky laminate to the price. A quick estimate of the total informed her the purchase would leave two dollars and eleven cents in her pocket.

"So can we? Can we?" Jayden pleaded, tapping the table with the heel of his hand. "We've been good all day, Aunt Cissy."

Good was an understatement. They hadn't uttered a peep when she'd been evicted that afternoon. *Evicted.* Cissy scoffed, turning to peer into the darkness outside the window.

So what? That seedy apartment wasn't fit to live in anyway. And she'd told the landlord so. The sleazy pig. She'd stabbed her finger two inches from his filthy mouth and advised him not to proposition the next female tenant. She might have the money to sue him.

Throwing her hands over her eyes, she groaned and slumped into her elbows on the table. Why did she have to do that? Her temper tended to cost her a lot of things, but a bed for the boys was too high a price.

After she'd unloaded on the landlord, there had been no choice but to stuff the boys, herself and the entirety of their possessions into her beat-up Toyota and leave. A quick pit stop for gas and they'd undertaken the journey from the busy interstates of Atlanta to the isolated stretches of Deep South Georgia roads.

Cissy rolled her eyes and dropped back against the thin padding of the booth. Things would've been okay if her cousin wasn't so dang irresponsible. Kip had promised them a place to stay. But when she'd banged on his door with a hungry twin on each arm and in desperate need of a restroom, there'd been no answer.

It wasn't until ten minutes later that he'd cracked the door open, drunk and disheveled. He was so sorry. He'd forgotten they were coming. He just needed a minute to get the room ready.

She'd been okay with that. Really. She had to be. Kip was the last bit of family she had left. And the boys needed a bed for the night. She had almost talked herself into it. Or she had, until a busty brunette had slumped in the doorway to coo at the boys, her curves barely concealed by the grimy sheet gripped against her.

One look at the woman's makeup-smeared face and slack expression had her clamping a hand over the boys' eyes and hauling them away again. No way was she exposing them to that! She'd find something else. She'd cut corners somewhere and they'd splurge on a motel room for a few nights.

But after driving six counties down, she had yet to find a motel. The drive had sucked away most of her money. And dinner would take almost every penny she had left. Her last emergency stash remained in the glove compartment. And it was tiny. Forget being able to pay for a motel room for more than one night.

"Please, Aunt Cissy." Kayden scowled.

"Mama woulda got us the triple burger if she was here," Jayden added, laying his cheek on the table. His eyelids sagged beneath the weight of the day.

A shaft of pain knifed her gut. She would have. Crystal would have moved heaven and earth for them. She always had. That was until cancer had taken over and she'd been unable to do anything for them. Or for herself.

Cissy's vision blurred. She'd lost half her soul the day they'd lowered her twin sister's coffin into the ground.

Oh, Crystal, how could you ever think I was up to this?

"Y'all ready to order?" A perky waitress smiled and propped a hand on her curvy hip.

Blinking hard, Cissy snapped the menu shut and nodded. "A triple-decker cheeseburger, onion rings and a hot fudge sundae." The boys squealed. "And could you cut the burger in half and bring an extra plate, too, please?"

Ms. Perky's smile widened. She winked as the boys bounced with excitement. "Of course. And for you?"

Cissy glanced down at the dregs lining her white mug. "Coffee refills are free, right?"

The smile wavered. "Well, yes, honey."

Forcing a bright smile of her own, Cissy passed her the metal condiment holder. "Then I'll take a refill and as many sugars as that'll hold. Thanks."

The smile slipped. "Sure thing, honey," the waitress murmured, lowering her eyes and carting the small container away.

Cissy lifted her chin. Lord, she really hated that look. That sad, woeful tilt of the lips. That sappy expression of pity. She should be used to it by now. But each time she found it stung even more than the time before.

"Aunt Cissy, look over there." Kayden pointed at a row of candy machines by the entrance. "They got—I mean, *they have*—jawbreakers."

"No, Kayden," she returned, rubbing a hand over her brow. "You're about to eat supper."

"But they're only twenty-five cents and you get two." His voice continued to rise. "Me and Jayden could save 'em for tomorrow."

Cissy's head throbbed, her patience thin. *Oh, for goodness' sakes.* What did a quarter matter now? Digging deep into her pocket, she dragged out a quarter between pinched fingers. Kayden plucked it from her almost before air hit it.

Moments later, the slap and bang of hands and feet on glass sounded.

"Boys." Cissy crouched around the side of the booth, shooting glances at the stares leveled on them. "Stop it."

"But it's stuck, Aunt Cissy," Jayden said, clenching his hands into small fists. "And it's got our quarter."

Cissy sucked her teeth and slid out of the booth. She grabbed the silver knob on the candy machine and gave it a few good turns.

"See. Told you," Jayden stated.

"Yeah, it's ripping you off, Aunt Cissy." Kayden stamped his foot.

"It's not ripping me off. And I'm not the one that had to have a jawbreaker anyway."

Truly reaching her breaking point, Cissy tightened her grip and twisted in rough jerks. The machine creaked and tilted forward on its loose pole with each of her efforts.

"Aw, she ain't gonna be able to do it. She's a girl." Kayden pouted.

Jayden nodded, looking disappointed.

"That's, she *will not* be able to do it," she corrected, "and I most certainly *will*."

Girl. That upped the stakes. She'd made it this far without help. Girl or not.

She braced her foot on the skinny pole connected to the base and gave the knob a vicious tug. Nothing.

Cissy's throat constricted. Maybe this was the last of many signs that she should have gone back. Returned the boys.

What had she expected? That her luck would suddenly change and things would go her way for once? She knew better than that. One thing she'd learned in her twenty-five years was to always keep expectations low. Yet, here she was thinking she could provide for the boys. That she could give them a better life than—

No. She wouldn't go down that road. It was out of the question. She'd made a promise to Crystal. And the only thing she had left of value was her word.

Gritting her teeth, Cissy bent over and yanked the handle toward her as she turned. She whooped as it gave a fraction of an inch. *Finally, a break.*

Petty or not, she paused to gloat. "See. I'm getting it."

She resumed the successful position and growled, her arms trembling under the strain. Heavy footfalls and a soft rush of wind at her upturned backside alerted her that someone approached. She pressed her foot harder into the pole and hopped forward a couple inches.

Good manners forced her to mutter a tight, "Excuse me."

A deep chuckle rumbled at her back. "Need a little help, ma'am?"

Cissy cut her eyes heavenward. *Great.* Just what she needed. Another testosterone-filled jerk.

"No, thank you," she grunted, her whole body tightening with effort.

"Oh, let him, Aunt Cissy. He's big. He can do it." Jayden's fingers tugged at her shirt, his eyes widening at the man behind her.

Tilting her chin up to the side, she found her eyes level with a large gold buckle, flat abs and thick thighs. She ripped her gaze away only for it to cling to the broad chest stretching a black T-shirt. Her mouth had gone dry by the time she made it past the man's chiseled jaw and sexy dimples, her attention landing on the sensual curve of his mouth. His grin widened, lifting his tanned cheeks. The dark pools of his chocolate-brown eyes sparkled.

"No," she choked, spinning back to her task. Tingles of awareness spread through her body, raising the tiny hairs on her arms.

She clamped down harder on the machine. No way was she going to play into this guy's hands. Well built, smug smile, knowing eyes… She knew the type.

Men. The second you had a menial task of no consequence, they abounded. But the minute you got yourself truly in a pickle, they were nowhere to be found. She squeezed her eyes shut as her irresponsible cousin sprang to mind.

Right. She could do this herself. She could do all of it. Obviously, Crystal had believed in her. It was time she began believing in herself. And the first order of business was to master this dang candy machine and get her quarter back.

As it was, she needed every penny she had.

Dominic Slade dragged his eyes away from the shapely bottom wiggling in front of him and knuckled his Stetson higher on his brow. A quick glance to his right reminded him the majority of male eyes in the room were also getting a good look. Only truckers and vagrants peppered the diner this time of night. He took a couple of steps forward, shifting his stance to shield the blonde from their gaze.

Not that he blamed them. He appreciated the curves of a woman as much as any other man, but he'd never ogle them in front of her kids. That was low.

Dominic sighed as his body demanded otherwise. He'd been on the road too long. He should've given in two states back and taken what the pretty redhead at the bar had offered. He should've accepted when she'd pressed a cold bottle of beer into his hand and her breasts against his biceps.

But he couldn't. Not after what the last morning-after had brought. Emptiness and regret. Self-recriminations and discontent. Part of what drove him back home was that feeling of reaching for something and never quite getting a grip on it. That and the thousandth guilt trip his brother had laid on him through the phone last week.

Brow creasing, he studied the woman as she struggled with the candy machine. Her attacks were relentless, the toned muscles in her pale arms and legs straining.

"Ma'am," he proffered, "why don't you let me give it a try?"

"No, I have it," she huffed. Her elbows jerked toward his gut, forcing him to take a step back.

Aw, hell. Nothing worse than a stubborn woman.

He turned to find the boys scrutinizing him. Their blond heads tilted to the side and wide blue eyes drifted down the length of him with slow precision. One of the carbon copies pursed his mouth as he seemed to come to a decision.

"Aunt Cissy." The boy's attention remained planted on him. "Let him. You're gonna break it."

Her grunt preceded, "No, I'm not, Kayden."

"Yes, you are," he reaffirmed.

The other copy cocked his head and nodded up at Dominic. "She is, you know."

Dominic shrugged. He should just walk away. Walking away would be nothing out of the norm for him. It would be expected, even.

Hell, the only reason he'd stopped in this hole in the wall to begin with was because they had the best burgers in a ten-state radius. Add to that, it was the last place he could catch his breath before the heavy press of home stifled it.

Besides, the quills on this gal's back could rival a porcupine. A man couldn't be blamed for self-preservation.

A high-pitched squeak cut through the air as the rubber sole of her scuffed shoe slipped off the pole. She regained her footing and bent deeper on a more ruthless attack. The hem of her denim shorts rose higher, exposing a greater expanse of smooth, creamy skin.

Dominic cast another look over his shoulder at the leering onlookers and gripped the back of his neck. The boys hovered off to the side, their faces clouded with doubt.

Hadn't he chosen to make this quick trip home with the intention of leaving on better terms? Maybe this was his first test. An opportunity to try being more responsible before his brother got a chance to cut into him.

Dominic stretched around her and touched the back of her hand with his palm. "Ma'am, you're not really getting anywhere—"

"I appreciate your offer but I'm doing just fine, thank you." She puffed a short strand of golden hair out of her face and glared up at him.

Damn. Those cornflower-blue eyes could bring a man to his knees. Or rip a gaping wound in his chest, which seemed to be her preference at the moment. He sprang to action as the candy machine took a sharp swing toward the boys.

"Now, look," he gritted, wrapping both arms around her trim waist to straighten the glass bowl, "this thing's about on its last leg—"

"I'm aware of that. If it wasn't, I wouldn't be in this predicament." She shoved her hip into his gut as the machine tottered on its stand.

"Y'all need some help?" A voice prompted from behind.

"No."

"Yes." Her shout outweighed his.

Dominic threw an apologetic look over his shoulder to find Sheila, a waitress he'd gotten to know too well on his last visit home, watching with trepidation.

"Well, Dom," Sheila squealed. She slapped her notepad against her apron, her gaze dropping south. "You're a sight for sore eyes."

Her stare penetrated the denim stretched over his backside. Yep. That night was high up on his list of regrets.

"Good to see you, Sheila," Dominic said, politeness spurring the lie.

He winced as an elbow thrust into his ribs, and turned to growl, "Let go and let me help you."

"You let go."

The words had barely escaped her mouth when he heard a sharp snap. She crashed back into his chest, toppling them both to the floor. Dominic had a split second of warning to roll her body under his before the candy-filled globe crashed at their side scattering glass and jawbreakers around them.

Yelps from the boys punctuated the sudden silence of the diner.

"Oh, Aunt Cissy, you broke it." One boy clapped his hands to his cheeks.

"I told you she was gonna break it." The other smirked, crossing his arms over his chest.

"You all right?" Dominic rasped, flexing his hand against the back of her head.

Her soft hair brushed his palm as she nodded. The tight press of her breasts against his chest sent a wave of heat through him. Clearing his throat, he surveyed her flushed face. Her blue eyes widened and her lush lips trembled.

Dominic bit back a grin. She sure packed a wallop

for such a tiny thing. Almost more than a few bulls he'd sat on recently. Except she was a helluva lot prettier. And a damned deal softer.

A subsequent crack issued from the remaining half of the machine. A metal piece banged to the floor and a rush of quarters poured out.

"She *really* broke it," the smug twin muttered with a disapproving shake of his head.

Dominic shifted his weight and rose to a kneeling position. The crack and crush of glass and candy erupted under each of his movements. Brushing debris off his boots, he proceeded to throw out a hand as the more outspoken twin moved toward them.

"Stay back," Dominic directed. "There's too much glass."

"Oh, I'm so sorry." Sheila clamped a hand to her ample chest. "That thing should've been replaced a long time ago."

Dominic opened his mouth to speak but the curvy bundle beneath him beat him to it.

"No, it was my fault." Issuing a soft apology, she pushed up on her elbows and made to rise.

"Wait." Dominic eyed the smooth skin of her thighs and calves. "You're gonna cut yourself."

Against his better judgment, he wrapped his arms around her again, obtained a firm foundation with his feet and lifted her up against his chest. He followed the shaky point of her finger to a nearby booth.

"Th-thanks," she stammered, brushing his hands away when they lingered a moment too long.

Nodding, he took refuge in assisting Sheila to sweep up the piles of broken glass and crushed candy.

Well, damn. Twenty minutes from home, he'd been

intent upon tossing a hot meal in his stomach, recovering from his last tour on the circuit and bolstering the courage to dig his feet into the dirt of his family's ranch again.

Instead, here he was, cleaning up a woman's mess. Something he'd been very careful to avoid over the years. So much for doing the right thing.

The back of his neck prickled, alerting him to the fact that the boys still observed him with interest. The soft hush of whispers and the shuffling of small feet around him solidified his suspicions.

"Hey, mister."

Dominic stilled his rough sweeping to look down. The more outspoken boy, who he recalled was named Kayden, barely reached his waist but jutted his chin out and eyed him with uncertainty.

"You a real cowboy?" he posed with all the seriousness of a sheriff.

A smile quirked Dominic's lips. "I've been accused of it before."

"He looks like one," Kayden's replica informed him in a stage whisper. "He's got a hat and boots."

Kayden pondered this for a moment, roving his gaze over Dominic once more. Locking eyes with him, he countered, "Yeah, but you got a horse?"

"Several," Dominic returned.

"A rope?" Kayden shot back.

"Yep."

"A gun?"

"Not on me." Dominic firmed his features. "They're dangerous, little man."

"He ain't got no dirt on his butt, Kayden," the other

twin exclaimed at his rear. "Real cowboys have dirty butts."

"Boys," their aunt shouted from the booth. "Stop that and get over here."

"Aw, come on, Aunt Cissy. We ain't never seen one up close before." Kayden rolled his lips and squinted at her.

"Well, you've seen one now, kiddos," Sheila interjected, dumping the last of the glass in the trash. "Dom here's not only a real cowboy but he's the top bull rider in the world. He's won the PBR championship four years in a row now." She ran her tongue over her bottom lip and smiled. "First ever to do it. Saw you on TV, Dom. You looked great."

Dominic issued a halfhearted smile. A scoff emerged from the direction of the booth. Turning, he watched the blonde blush and tilt her chin higher.

"That where you got *this*?" Kayden popped a fist into his belt buckle, coming dangerously close to sensitive parts of his anatomy.

Dominic recoiled. "Whoa, there."

"That's it." Their aunt's blue eyes spat sparks. "Get over here now." She jabbed a finger toward the floor and pinned the boys with a stern look. They reluctantly complied, dragging their feet over to hop up beside her in the booth.

"I'm really sorry about this." Sheila divested him of the broom and passed her eyes over each of them. "Meal's on the house. Dom, what can I get you?"

He opened his mouth to respond when Kayden piped, "We got a triple cheeseburger. That's what you should get."

He laughed at the boy's authoritative tone. It'd been

a long time since he'd been around a kid. He forgot how lively they could make a mundane event.

"Sounds good," Dominic said. "I'll have it with fries." He ambled toward a bar stool but drew up short when Kayden waved a small hand in his direction.

"Hey, come sit with us. There's room," Kayden urged with an eager expression.

He hated to disappoint the boy but was willing to. Dominic was about to decline, but found the words sticking in his throat when their aunt shushed the boy then shot a look of disapproval his way.

Dominic grunted. *Fine thanks for trying to help someone out.* "You know what?" He threw a smile in the boys' direction. "Don't mind if I do."

He maneuvered his big frame into the other side of the booth, sucking in his abs and wobbling the table forward a few inches to make more room. Removing his hat, he placed it on the edge of the table and dragged a hand through his hair.

The look of irritation flitting across her delicate features widened his smile. Now, this was something new. It'd been a long time since he had to work to get the attention of a woman.

"Here you go." Sheila plopped two plates of food and a tray of sugar packets in front of the trio. "And, Dom," she purred, setting a meal in front of him. Hesitating, she cast a glance at the boys' aunt. "You sure I can't get you anything more? It's gratis. Soup? Pie?"

"No, thank you." She refused to look up and helped the boys arrange napkins in their laps.

No surprise there. She was probably one of those women that lived off salad and diet soda. Dominic dug into his food with almost as much gusto as the boys.

It'd been several days since he'd stopped long enough to sit somewhere and let his stomach settle.

"Cissy, huh?" he mumbled out around a bite of burger before dragging a napkin across his mouth.

He noticed her eyes followed the movement and lingered on his lower lip. She wasn't completely unaffected by him. Dominic dropped his gaze to the table to hide his satisfaction.

"Cissy," she affirmed. "Cissy Henley."

"I'm Kayden," the boy garbled out around his own mouthful of food.

"And this is Jayden," Cissy commented, nodding in the other boy's direction.

He swallowed before taking another huge bite and offering up his own introduction. "Dominic Slade."

"Cowboy." A bit of food flew out of Jayden's mouth at the declaration and Cissy quickly admonished them both not to talk with their mouths full.

Abashed, Dominic pressed his lips together and chewed, making sure his mouth was empty before asking, "Y'all from around here?"

"No" was her only response before taking a gulp of coffee.

Though Cissy seemed intent upon drinking, her long lashes lifted and she returned her attention to his mouth.

Dominic's blood rushed as her eyes darkened. He shifted in the small confines of the booth, uncomfortably aware of the tightness of his jeans. He damned sure had been on the road too long.

Cissy lowered the cup and continued to stare. Surely she wasn't trying to come on to him in front of the kids. Not that it'd be the first time. Lately, nothing women did surprised him.

Thankful for the silence that ensued, Dominic continued working on his meal. He was impressed by the boys' appetites. They managed to polish off each half of their burger, every onion ring and almost an entire sundae. Only a few drops of melted ice cream remained.

Jayden flopped back with a sigh. "I'm full."

"Me, too," Kayden added. Their eyes were heavy and they looked as though they could nod off at any moment.

"I should hope so," Dominic commented with a chuckle, the last third of his burger hovering above his plate between his fingertips. "Don't know where you two possibly put it all."

That drew a sleepy but broad smile from them both.

"We're bottomless pits," Jayden piped with pride, tapping his chest with his fist.

Cissy laughed and ruffled her fingers through their blond hair. The boys closed their eyes and leaned into her, soaking it up and drifting off. Dominic couldn't help but admire her expression. Her whole face lit up, her eyes bright.

As though sensing his scrutiny, she faced him again and nibbled on the rosy curve of her bottom lip. His stomach flipped over at her shy look. She had freckles. They were scattered over the bridge of her pert nose and the apples of her cheeks. He had the strange urge to touch his tongue to them to see if they tasted as sweet as they looked.

"Dominic?" she asked, leaning forward. Her tongue curled around his name. She carefully moved her arms from the sleeping boys and slid them across the table. Her breasts pressed against the edge.

Dominic peeled his eyes from the scoop of her white

tank top and cursed himself for wishing the neckline was a good bit lower. "Yeah?" he choked.

"Are you finished?" A flush of pink heat encompassed her cheeks, obscuring the freckles.

He stilled. This was it. Proposition time. He had to give her points, though. She'd put it off a lot longer than most women. And despite his cynicism, he surprised himself by being eager to play.

"Are you finished?" she repeated with a raised brow. Those beautiful blues of hers moved from his mouth to his hand.

"Yeah," he mumbled.

She drew closer, stretching across the distance between them, and lifted her hand. His body tightened and his eyelids lowered to half-mast as he anticipated her touch on his skin.

"Great," she chimed.

Empty air drifted between his fingers. Dominic frowned. He'd been robbed.

Cissy stuffed a good portion of what remained of his triple cheeseburger into her mouth and closed her eyes. Mustard trickled off the side of her chin and her pink tongue shot out to catch it with a low moan of pleasure.

Well, double damn. This was definitely a first.

A loud ring jarred from underneath the table. Cissy jumped, then scrambled around, producing a cell phone before quickly silencing it and shoving it back in her pocket.

"Fwanks," she mumbled around the wad of burger. "We gotta glo."

"But…"

Dominic blinked, struggling to get a grip on the situation when she rose from her seat and jostled the boys awake. She tugged money from her pocket, counted out a few bills and dropped them onto the table. The remnants of hot desire pumped through his veins as she bustled the boys out of the booth.

She stooped to grab a quarter from the pile still resting on the floor where the candy machine used to reside. Her eyes brushed over him, dismissing him and focusing on the exit just before she tugged the boys out the door.

Dominic shifted at the uncomfortable churn in his gut. *What the hell just happened?*

"You finished, Dom?"

Sheila's perky voice grated across his nerves as he strained to make out the trio in the darkness beyond the window. Cissy leaned into the backseat of a battered Toyota and strapped the boys in with one hand. The other still held the last bit of his burger.

"Yeah," he stated offhandedly, watching as Cissy finished settling the boys and polished off the last bite, pausing as she reached the driver's-side door.

"Poor thing," Sheila observed. "I got the feeling she couldn't afford to buy herself something to eat. She made sure those boys got what they wanted, though. Cute kids but a bit rowdy."

Frowning, Dominic examined the stiff line of Cissy's back. She stared to her right at the long stretch of highway before turning her head to the left and peering equally as hard.

"Did she mention where they were headed?" He delivered the question through stiff lips.

He traveled light. The last thing he needed was a complication. Much less three of them.

"Nope. She wasn't the talkative type." Sheila pressed

against his side and asked, "Anything else I can get you?"

Forced to pull his attention from the window, he drudged up a polite smile. "No, thanks." He withdrew a hefty tip from his pocket and dropped it on the table before rising. "It was good running into you."

"Anytime, *cowboy*," she mocked with humor. "Give me a call if you get bored later."

Dominic ducked his heated face in acknowledgment before leaving. Stepping outside, he watched the battered Toyota groan its way up the graveled drive and take a right.

Travel light. He slapped his hat against his leg then settled it back on his head with the firm reminder. He already had his hands full with returning home. He should get in his truck and go straight to the ranch. No stops. Straight there. Put in an appearance, shake his brother off his back then get on the road as planned.

Cissy's plight wasn't any of his business. And it was clear she didn't want him to have any part of it. She couldn't have made it any plainer when she'd looked right through him as though he wasn't there.

As though he was nothing.

But that was to be expected. Out here, he was no one's hero. Dominic grimaced. Except maybe Sheila's.

He strolled to his truck and gripped the hard metal of the door handle only to find his gaze straying back to the highway and the fast-dwindling taillights of Cissy's car.

Damn. It would've been worth one more regretful night to wake up with that sexy spitfire draped over him. To look down at those beautiful blues of hers in the bright light of day.

Dominic sighed and jerked the door open. *Travel light.* After a quick visit home, he'd return to the circuit where he measured up. And the sooner, all the damn better.

Chapter Two

The steering wheel pulled hard to the right, jerking Cissy's hands with it. Tugging on the wheel, she straightened the car and coaxed it forward again. Twelve minutes after bailing the greasy diner and her ragged car was dying on the highway.

A loud hum from her cell phone sounded over the clanking of the engine. *Persistent joker!* That was one thing she had to give Jason Reed, the twins' father, credit for. Once he got his mind set on something, he was like a pit bull. He'd sink his teeth in and never let go.

The vibrating stopped. Cissy bit her lip and hunched against the steering wheel. Her heart lurched. Sweat streamed from her brow, burning the corner of her eye.

Real stupid, Cissy. Stupid, stupid, stupid. What had she done? What was she thinking packing the boys up and dragging them all over the state of Georgia?

The cell phone, though silent, seared through the pocket of her shorts, scorching its presence into her thigh. She relinquished her clutch on the steering wheel and readjusted it with trembling fingers.

Okay. She'd screwed up again. Big-time. Lost her temper. Her home. Her direction in life.

Wrapping her hands tighter around the wheel, she willed the car on. It didn't have to be as bad as it seemed. All she needed to do was buy some time and find a bit of work to tide them over until she found something permanent.

And she would. She always managed to pull through.

Her chest tightened. Only, it had always been just her. It wasn't just her anymore. She had two children to consider now. And the damage was already done. What was she going to do?

Cissy swallowed hard and renewed her grip on the steering wheel. A motel was probably right over the next hill. Just a few more miles.

"Come on, ol' girl," she cajoled, patting the dash.

A loud pop and a sharp jerk of the steering wheel had her gasping as the car veered off the road and jerked to a stop.

"What's wrong, Aunt Cissy?" Jayden mumbled.

Squaring her shoulders, she mentally directed herself to calm down and glanced in the backseat. Jayden was struggling to keep his eyes open. Kayden had long since been out for the count and sprawled with snoring abandon in his booster seat.

"Nothing, baby," she whispered. "Go back to sleep."

Nothing? She yanked the keys out of the ignition. That was the understatement of the year. Or, at least, the biggest lie she'd ever told. It was pitch-black outside. They'd just blown a tire. She was sure of it. And, now they were stranded on the edge of a ditch, in the middle of nowhere, without a soul in sight.

Cissy dug out a flashlight from the glove compartment and went to survey the damage. The low beam glowed over a deflated heap of rubber pooling on the grass. It was a lost cause.

She rotated to take in her surroundings, the flash-light bouncing in her shaky grip. There were no houses or driveways. The dim light flickered over wire fences and the edges of empty fields. Only menacing dark-ness lay beyond.

Cissy dropped her head and kicked the ground. How irresponsible could she be? She'd panicked and taken a chance without weighing it first. She'd jumped without a net, and instead of landing on her feet she was plum-meting facedown toward the dirt.

What should she do now? What would Crystal do?

Her mouth twisted. Crystal would never have gotten the boys into a mess like this to begin with. Her sister may have been weak in the head where Jason was con-cerned but she would never have taken such a gamble on their security. She would've sweet-talked any sleazy landlord if it meant keeping a roof over the boys' heads.

Cissy slapped the flashlight against her palm. Heck if she'd do that. She'd never beg a slimeball like him for charity.

Keep our boys together, Cissy. Crystal's plea whis-pered in her mind and wrapped around her on the humid summer air. *Give them what we never had. Promise me...*

And she had promised.

A salty tang hit Cissy's mouth, tears settling in the corners. Licking them away, she blinked hard and dragged the back of her hand over her cheeks.

Fat lot of good it would do to stand here and cry by the side of the road all night. She had to think. She had to focus.

She shoved the flashlight into her back pocket, then flipped on the hazard lights, and then leaned against the trunk. Moments later, the rumble of an engine rattled the dinky car at her back. Bright lights emerged over the hill and flooded her face.

She threw an arm up to shield her eyes as the loud truck drew to a halt. A large male frame emerged from the truck's cab and positioned itself in front of the headlights. Uneasiness seeped into her gut.

"Hey!" Cissy shouted over the growling vehicle.

The silhouette placed its hands on its hips and the outline of a Stetson dipped in response.

"You want to shut that thing off? It'll just about make a person deaf, you know?"

No response.

Crap. She squinted against the lights and dropped her arm to adopt a more defensive stance. "Look, I have a flat. Is there a tow-truck service around here?"

The figure took a few steps toward her but didn't answer.

Great. Just great. Now some psycho redneck was going to butcher her and toss her body parts in the ditch. She reached around her back and gripped the end of the flashlight.

"Hey, I asked you a question." Her heart pounded as he drew closer. She snatched the flashlight out of her back pocket and threw out a hand. "Stop."

He didn't. He just kept on coming. Adrenaline shot through her veins. She cast a quick look over her shoulder to the backseat, glancing at the boys' blond heads illuminated by the headlights.

"I said stop." Cissy jerked her arm over her head and

flung the flashlight, clenching her fists in victory when it thumped against the silhouette's head.

"Ow! Dammit," the voice boomed as the figure folded over.

She almost collapsed with relief at the familiar tenor. "Dominic."

He shifted closer, blocking the headlights and bringing his face into view. A bright red lump was appearing right below the brim of his hat. "What are you trying to do? Kill me?"

"I'm sorry. I didn't know it was you." She slumped back against the car. "You shouldn't have walked up on me like that. You scared the crap out of me."

Dominic removed his hat, rubbing a hand over his brow and through his hair. The midnight strands fell forward in tousled waves.

"Good," he growled, settling the Stetson back on his head. "You should be scared. You never stand outside your vehicle like that. You're just asking for someone to snatch you up."

Cissy lifted her chin and dragged her attention away from his dark eyes. "Well, seems to me like you wouldn't have had much success in *snatching me up*, as you put it."

Dominic grunted. He retrieved the flashlight from the ground, shoved it into her hand then banded his blunt fingers around her wrist. "What were you gonna do if this thing missed? Kick my kneecaps? You're too short to reach much else."

"Actually, I had something higher in mind," she smirked, spinning the flashlight with her fingers.

Dominic's luscious mouth twitched. He flattened it and rolled his eyes. "Right."

Releasing her, he moved his muscular girth past her to survey the flat. A drift of spicy maleness enveloped her. *Good Lord, he smelled good.*

Fingers trembling, she rolled the flashlight between her palms. The heat from his grip still lingered on the base and she found her fingertips returning to smooth over it.

"You got a spare?"

"You're looking at it."

Releasing a heavy sigh, he leaned down and glanced inside the backseat. "They been out long?"

"Since we left the diner. They've had a long day."

He nodded and opened the door. "I'll get this one, you grab the other one."

"Wait a minute." She rushed over to stall him with a hand on his arm. Ignoring the bulk of his biceps under her fingers, she demanded, "What do you think you're doing?"

"The only thing there is to do. Loading them in my truck and taking them somewhere to sleep." His tone turned mocking. "Or do you expect me to leave y'all stranded by the side of the road in the middle of the night?"

Cissy frowned. "No. But I don't really know you. You're a stranger."

His black eyebrows rose. She had to agree with him. Her choice of words was lame.

"A stranger?" Dominic's lip hitched. "I wasn't so strange earlier when you stole my half-eaten burger outta my hand." His eyes softened as he ran them over her face. "These boys are too young to sleep in a car by the side of the road. It's not safe. You have to admit that."

She opened her mouth but couldn't manage to issue a sound. The summer heat engulfed her skin, rolling a drop of sweat between her breasts.

Spearing a hand through her hair, she flicked her eyes over the empty darkness surrounding them. What choice did she have? As much as she hated admitting it, he was right. The boys needed to be settled for the night.

Dominic nodded at her silence, then turned back to the car's interior to unbuckle Jayden's seat belt.

"Wait." Cissy shot in front of him and gathered Jayden up in her arms. Maintaining her position, she clutched him to her chest and clenched her jaw.

Dominic's mouth tightened and he took a step back. If he was offended, he didn't comment on it. He just watched her for a handful of seconds then shrugged.

"Okay," he said. "I'll grab their car seats. They'll fit in the cab. Once the boys are settled, we'll toss your bags in the back."

They did so, with Cissy keeping a close eye on Dominic as he helped settle Jayden in the truck. They made swift work of relocating Kayden and the bags, too, and soon pulled out onto the road again.

"What about my car?" Cissy twisted in the passenger seat to watch it fade into the darkness.

"We'll see about it in the morning. Get the tire replaced." He paused as they turned onto a dirt road. "Although, from the looks of it, it needs a lot more than just a tire."

She shot him a dirty look. Yeah. It did need a lot more than that. But a polite person wouldn't have pointed it out.

That wasn't the worst of it, though. She couldn't afford a new tire. Or anything else, for that matter. Licking her lips, she turned her face away to look out of the window. Better to keep that bit of information to herself for now.

"Y'all were packed tight in there. Where were you headed?"

They bounced around as a pothole jostled them. Cissy glanced over her shoulder to find the boys still sleeping. "Nowhere in particular. I was just looking for the next motel."

Dominic grunted. "Well, you weren't gonna find one on that road for a while. Only thing for the next couple hours' drive would've been deer and cemeteries."

They hit another bump and Cissy reached back to prop Kayden's dangling hand back in his lap. The action brought her face close to Dominic's arm and she couldn't prevent herself from taking a second look at the sinewy length. Even his forearm was defined, the toned tendons accentuated with a sprinkling of black hair.

And his scent was everywhere. That mix of sandalwood and man permeated every inch of the truck's upholstery and released into the air with each of his movements. She forced herself to refocus on the boys and reached back to move a lock of hair off Jayden's forehead.

"It's just y'all?" His sexy rumble warmed her belly.

She met his sharp look for a moment before facing the window again. "Yeah."

She strained to see beyond the halo of the truck's headlights. It was too dark to see much other than the billowing of dust from the bottom of the truck and the passing of fence posts.

"Where's their mama?"

Cissy clutched her hands in her lap and focused

ahead on the uneven line of grass that met the dirt path they traveled. "Gone."

"Their dad?"

She stilled her nervous movements and remained silent.

Her skin prickled at the sweep of his dark gaze on her once more. She bit her lip. He didn't pursue it. Leaning her head back against the headrest, she welcomed the silence in the cab.

A few minutes later, he slowed the truck as they turned into a gated entrance. The truck's headlights illuminated a wooden sign etched with the name Raintree Ranch as they proceeded.

"Raintree?" She vaguely recalled that tiny dot on the map she'd used.

"Yep."

"This is your ranch?"

His mouth twisted. "Partially."

Cissy drew up at his cynical tone and returned her attention to the windshield. The dirt road dipped and curved past a mammoth barn, dark paddocks and a dimly lit pond before leading them to an almost palatial house. She caught a glimpse of white columns, wide windows and several stories before the truck continued past and halted at the end of a back driveway.

"Let's get the boys inside," Dominic directed as he hopped out. Her hesitancy must have shown on her face. He leaned back into the cab to point out, "You can't carry them both, Cissy."

At her nod, he unloaded Jayden, hoisted him on his hip and led the way up a narrow path to a back door. She followed closely behind, clutching Kayden to her chest and stepping with care past the azaleas on each side of the walkway. The boys issued small grunts as they were jostled about and began lifting their heads as Dominic banged on the door.

"It's really late, Dominic," she said. "Don't you have a key?"

He turned to study her for a moment. "Somewhere. Haven't needed it in a while."

Raising his big fist, he banged again. A light came on and one of the doors burst open.

A voice thundered, "What the hell, Dom?"

"I'm not alone, Logan," Dominic bit out.

Cissy lifted to her toes, peering over Dominic's broad shoulder. She just caught the angry frown of a tall, disheveled man. Shifting his weight, Dominic brought Jayden fully into the man's line of sight.

Her stomach turned over and she clutched Kayden closer to her chest. It was much too late for visitors. She wouldn't blame the guy—*Logan, was it?*—if he shooed them off and slammed the door.

Dominic's bulk moved forward and she followed in his wake. Crossing the threshold, she stopped and glanced at Logan. There was a remarkable resemblance to Dominic, although this man was leaner and the lines on his face were slightly deeper.

His eyes were tired. Cissy winced. He probably thought she was an insensitive jerk for ripping him from his bed. She opened her mouth to issue an apology but he spoke first.

"Sorry. I didn't see the boys." Logan's eyes swept the length of her, pausing to scrutinize Kayden's face. "Please come in."

"Thank you." She lowered her chin to rest it on Kayden's soft hair as she proceeded inside.

She kept close to Dominic's heels, noting the kitchen was larger than the last three apartments she'd lived in put together. Granite countertops gleamed, stainless-steel appliances lined every wall and several oak tables were stationed about.

"Here," Dominic instructed, pulling a chair out with his foot. "Have a seat. If you'll hold on to them for a minute, I'll get a room ready."

Cissy lowered into the chair, adjusting Kayden onto her left hip as Dominic maneuvered Jayden onto the right one. Their legs dangled off on either side and she wrapped her arms tighter around them.

"Got 'em?" Dominic's big, tanned hand hovered above Jayden's back.

She looked down and readjusted the boys. Her scuffed sneakers were a marked contrast with the polished hardwood floor. She slid them underneath her chair.

"Yeah." Her face flamed.

Dominic stepped away. "I'll be back in a minute."

Logan cast one last look at the boys before leaving the room. Closing her eyes, Cissy sighed. Wisps of the boys' hair moved and tickled her chin. She dropped her cheek to the top of their heads, rubbing it back and forth.

How had they ended up here? And in the middle of the night with an almost stranger?

She cringed. There was no way she could pay for her car being towed, a new tire and room and board for the night. What would Logan and Dominic do when they found out she was broke and had no place to go? Would they throw them out? Or worse, call Family and Children Services?

Clutching the boys tighter to her chest, she whispered an apology when Jayden whimpered. "It's okay. Everything's gonna be okay."

And if it wasn't, she'd make it okay.

The cell phone in her pocket buzzed against her thigh. Cissy's hands curled tighter around the boys. The incessant vibrations persisted despite her attempts to ignore them.

Keep our boys together, Cissy.

She firmed her features. She'd make it okay. She had to.

"Are they yours?"

"Hell, no," Dominic spat.

He winced at the harsh words that burst from his mouth. The warmth from Jayden's body still lingered on his right side. And it wasn't the kids' fault his brother had turned into a cynical ass.

It was just like Logan to come out with guns blazing. This was the exact reason he'd put off coming home for so long this time out. Dominic gritted his teeth and flicked his eyes over the room to rein in his temper.

Not much had changed in Raintree Ranch's main office over the past year and a half. It remained organized, controlled and presentable. Just like Logan.

Shoving his fists into his pockets, Dominic stared his brother down. "Those boys have to be at least five. For God's sake, Logan, is that what you think of me? That I'd abandon my own flesh and blood for the first years of their life?"

"I don't know, Dom," Logan returned, eyes piercing into his. "You just hit twenty-five. And you sure as hell left a trail in your wake. You probably don't know what you've left behind."

Dominic straightened. "Oh, I'd know. That's one chance I don't take."

Logan maintained his stance behind the mahogany desk. Hands flat on the counter, head lifted. "Mistakes happen."

"Yeah," Dominic sneered, "and don't you know it, big bro?"

That got a reaction.

Logan shoved off the desk, rounding it and bringing his face so close it blurred. "If you came home just to stir shit up, you can haul your ass off right now. Don't have time for it. Some of us work for a living."

"And I don't?" Dominic jerked his chin up. "Whose work produced the money to build this place to begin with?"

"I wouldn't call getting thrown on your back by bulls and buckle bunnies actual work." Logan stepped away and narrowed his eyes. "But heaven forbid we ever forget that you still cut us a check every month." His brows rose. "Want to see 'em? I haven't been cashing them. Just stacking them up all nice and neat in a pile and locking them in the safe so you'll have proof you did your part when the time comes."

Dominic's gut roiled. "You're a real bastard when you want to be, Logan."

"Yeah," he said, nodding, "and you love it. Makes it real easy to sweep back in here and be the charming hero every couple years. Tell me, how many times did you call Pop over the past year and a half?"

Dominic spun around, then strode to the window and hunched his shoulders. "He has you."

"He sees me every day, you know? It's not me he wants to talk to. It's you." Logan's scornful laugh crossed the room to grate over his ears. "Don't worry. He won't hold it against you. He never does."

"Where is he?"

"Where do you think? It's after eleven at night. This is a working guest ranch. We get up at the crack of dawn here. We don't wallow around until noon recovering from parties the night before."

Shame washed over Dominic, burning his neck. This was going nowhere.

Yanking his fists free, he stalked across the room. "You think you can put this in your back pocket until morning? I'm not feeling it right now and those kids out there are 'bout dead on their feet. All I need is a room key and I'll be out of your hair for a few hours."

Logan sighed then moved back behind the desk. He yanked a drawer open and rustled through it before holding out a key. "Twenty-seven's the only one empty. Has a king-size bed and en suite bathroom. It's on the second floor."

"I know where it is. I haven't been gone *that* long."

"I assume you plan on staying in the bunkhouse as usual."

The bunkhouse. Away from the main house. Away from Logan's stifling grip. *Hell, yes.*

"You assume right." Dominic swiped the key out of Logan's hand and jerked his wallet free from his back pocket to produce a wad of bills. Tossing them down, he jeered, "Brought cash this time instead of a check. Throw that on the pile."

His boots landed with thuds on the wood floor as he stomped away.

"Dom?"

A softening in Logan's tone halted him. Dominic tilted his head but didn't turn around.

"Stay awhile this time, yeah?"

Dominic looked over his shoulder. Logan's expression was still carved in stone, but his eyes pleaded with Dom's.

"We'll see," he murmured.

A tremor tore through his frame at the gruff sound of his voice. It was just exhaustion. He'd been on the road too long and he needed to recuperate. And he needed to get those boys settled before he did that.

Jerking away, he returned to the kitchen, drawing to a halt in the doorway. The boys were still knocked out, their limbs draped around Cissy. Her cheek rested on top of their heads and their bodies lifted and lowered with each soft breath that passed between her parted lips. The blond sweep of her hair had fallen to one side and settled in a silken pool on one of the boy's shoulders.

Her expression was softer. No angry scowl or judgmental glare. Sleep had claimed her, too.

Dominic grinned. She sure was a lot less temperamental in this state. And even in her sleep, her arms were like steel bands wrapped around those boys. It was obvious she cared for them.

The grin vanished as his gut churned. Still, having kids didn't always mean someone stuck around. He'd found that out first hand. Unlimited funds and fun was all it had taken to lure his mother away. He'd learned a long time ago that everyone had their price. And expectations.

Rolling his shoulders, he shrugged off the unpleasant thoughts and refocused on their peaceful faces.

Well, damn. He couldn't carry all of them up the stairs. He'd have to wake her. He moved with soft steps across the room then lowered to his haunches at her feet.

"Cissy," he whispered. He ran his eyes over the freckles scattered across the bridge of her nose. Unable to resist, he touched the pad of his thumb to them and drifted it over the soft skin of her exposed cheek. His tanned hand stood out in stark contrast to her porcelain complexion.

Her eyes popped open and she lifted her head. Beet-red heat covered her other cheek. It glistened with sweat and the boys' hair stuck to it.

"Hey." He bit back a smile. "I got a room for you. Think you can make it up a flight of stairs?"

Blinking hard, she shifted upright and nodded. "Yeah."

"There was only one open." He lifted Jayden from her and arranged the boy on his hip. No response. These boys were like the dead when they slept. "It's only got one bed but should be big enough for all of you."

"I'm sure it'll be fine."

Her voice was husky with sleep. It whispered over him and stirred a deep ache. He forced himself to concentrate on the task at hand.

"Well, come on and I'll take you up."

Leading the way up the winding staircase, he kept a firm hand on Jayden's back, glancing back at Cissy every few feet. She held Kayden close, but the boy's weight seemed to take a toll on her, slowing her steps and weighing her small frame down.

"This is it." Dominic unlocked the door, opened it a

crack and waited for her to reach his side. "No chance they're gonna be up and about anymore tonight. I'll bring your bags in tomorrow morning if you can do without them till then."

She puffed a gold strand of hair out of her eyes. "That's fine."

He toed the door open and moved to the bed, depositing Jayden on one side. Cissy followed and laid Kayden down, as well. Dominic stepped back, hands hanging at his sides.

Cissy's hip brushed his when she leaned in to untie and remove Kayden's shoes. Her shirt rose from the waistband of her shorts, revealing smooth, silky skin. Dominic stifled the urge to run his palm over it and focused on her slim hands as she peeled off Kayden's socks.

Seeking a distraction, Dominic did the same for Jayden and dropped the items in a pile by the bed.

The boy's head was at an awkward angle, his mouth open and snoring. Dominic smirked. He'd passed out in the same position on many occasions. And nine times out of ten woke with a kink in his neck. Better head that off at the pass.

Reaching down, Dominic shifted Jayden's head to a more comfortable position and started when his eyes fluttered open. Jayden blinked several times before a slow smile stretched across his face, his eyelids heavy and drooping.

"Cowboy," Jayden whispered. His small hand fluttered upward to grasp the leather cord of the choker dangling from Dominic's neck. Curling his fingers around it, he tugged hard.

Dominic lowered his head, easing the pull of the

cord around his neck and bringing his face close to the boy's. Jayden's other hand rose to bump and glide over the stubble on his jaw, his tiny palm warm and sweaty against his cheek.

"You'll be here when I wake up?" Jayden's words emerged soft and slurred. He was already drifting back off.

Dominic's chest tightened and his face flushed. For sure, he'd be here tomorrow. Beyond that, it was anyone's guess.

Jayden's sleepy gaze clung to him, hopeful expectancy glowing on his face.

"Yeah, buddy," Dominic whispered.

Gently untangling Jayden's fingers, he laid the boy's arms back on the bed and stepped back. The weight of Cissy's stare pressed on his face. He averted his head and moved awkwardly toward the door.

"Dominic?"

Rubbing his hands over his jeans, he turned. Cissy's hair was mussed and her eyes shadowed but her voice rang clear.

"Yeah?"

"Thanks for this."

Her hands twisted at her waist, pulling on her thin shirt. There was a small wet spot on the material. It clung to the upper curve of her breast where Kayden's face had rested.

She looked vulnerable, lost and alone.

His palms itched to reach out and pull her in. Tuck her head beneath his chin and hold her close. He stepped forward.

She reached him first, pressing her fingertips against

his chest and propelling him toward the door. "Good night," she whispered.

The warmth from her fingers spread throughout his body as she nudged him into the hall. The soft fall of her blond hair and curve of her rosy cheek disappeared behind the firm click of the closed door.

The warmth dissipated, leaving cold emptiness behind. Dominic ran his palm over the smooth wood. Straining, he listened to the faint rustlings as she moved around the room.

A wry grin crept across his mouth and a low laugh escaped. "Well...*damn*."

It was the first time a woman had ever shown him the door. And, for the first time, he wanted nothing more than to get back on the other side of it.

Chapter Three

It was too still. Too quiet.

"Boys?" Cissy called out.

She smoothed an arm out to her side, sighing with pleasure at the coolness of the sheet. Her fingers crept over the lumps and bumps of the bedding before bumping into the bulk of a pillow. She cracked her eyes open to find a deep impression in the down where a head had burrowed the night before.

Bolting upright, she found the other side of the bed empty, as well. A quick scan of the room revealed the same. The only sign of the boys' presence from the night before were the creases and folds left in the linen.

Her heart pounded. "Boys?"

She dropped over the side of the bed, dipping her head and finding the floor empty. There were no giggles or whispers of mischief from hidden spaces. They weren't hiding.

They were gone.

Cissy scrambled out of the bed. She shot to the door and flung it open, stumbling to a stop in the hallway.

Over six feet of rock-solid muscle and a throaty purr met her at the door. "Morning."

Dominic tipped his dark head in greeting, then resumed his relaxed stance against the opposing wall. The soft fabric of his T-shirt stretched across the bulge of his chest as he crossed his burly arms.

"Where are the boys?" Could he hear the breathlessness in her voice? She hoped not.

Her stomach flipped over at his lopsided grin. *Damn the man*. It was downright sinful for a guy to look this good on a Sunday morning.

"Right there." He nodded to his left.

Kayden stood at the end of the hall, feet planted wide apart, swinging a lasso over his head. Jayden stood motionless a few feet away, his face contorted with apprehension.

"You ain't doing it right," Jayden warned.

"Aw, just be still," Kayden said, twirling the lasso with more gusto.

"You gave Kayden a rope?" Cissy shuddered at the images that popped into her mind.

Turning, she caught Dominic's gaze transfixed to the top of her head. He rolled in his full bottom lip and stifled a smile.

"What?" Cissy glared, searching his face.

He held on to his silence, shaking his head. The smile he fought reemerged. Dimples broke out on both lean cheeks and his dark eyes crinkled at the corners.

Men. She'd given up trying to figure out their thought process a long time ago.

"Look." She ground her teeth together. "I appreciate you giving us a room for the night but I don't want you taking the boys off without me *or* my permission."

"Wasn't a way around that this morning." Dominic turned to study the boys. "They ventured out before the crack of dawn. Needed something to do. And I didn't want to wake you."

She followed his line of sight to the boys and winced as Kayden slung the rope with bad aim. It smacked against the side of Jayden's face and rebounded, knocking against a picture on the wall and clanging it to the floor.

"Ouch!" Jayden rushed over and shoved his brother. "I told you you weren't doing it right."

"Boys," Cissy shouted, "stop that and get over here."

They both jumped at her voice and spun, bounding down the hall toward her. Kayden halted a foot away and burst into laughter.

"Aunt Cissy, you got a Mohawk," he cackled.

She jerked her eyes upward. A few clumps of hair stood on end above her forehead, waving slightly with her movements. *Oh, for goodness' sakes.* She'd been in such a panic to find the boys she hadn't bothered to comb the rats' nest.

Face burning, she groaned and dropped her eyes to her wrinkled shirt. She'd worn her clothes from yesterday to bed, and they were rumpled almost beyond recognition. And she'd torn out of the room in such a hurry she'd left her shoes behind.

This had to be a nightmare. She wiggled her unpolished toes against the gleaming hardwood floor just to be sure she was awake.

"Here," Kayden called. A sharp tug on Cissy's wrist had her at eye level. "I'll fix it."

"No, Kayden, wait."

Dominic's deep tenor and heavy footsteps registered right before Kayden jabbed his hand in her hair, fingers snarling in her bangs.

"Ow." Cissy grabbed his wrist and yanked, but something sticky snagged every strand.

"It's the syrup," Dominic whispered softly into her ear as he gently untangled Kayden's hand. "They just had pancakes."

She peeked at him from the corners of her eyes. His chiseled jaw was fresh shaven and the soft scent of soap and detergent accompanied each of his movements. His deep chuckle rumbled at her side, the heat of his palm caressing her scalp sending a thrill down her spine.

"Thanks," Cissy mumbled. She stepped away and smoothed a shaky hand over her matted hair.

"The pancakes were awesome, Aunt Cissy." Jayden reached her side and wound his sticky fingers through hers. "Ms. Betty cooked some for you, too."

"Ms. Betty?" Cissy couldn't help but smile at his excited expression.

"Head chef," Dominic answered for him. "Though she refuses the title. Ms. Betty's been heading up the meals here for years."

Cissy nodded, eyeing Kayden. His knuckles tightened around the rope, wiggling the end that trailed along the floor. She stooped, grabbed it with her free hand and tugged.

"Have you been torturing your brother with this all morning?"

"No," Kayden said, pulling.

Cissy narrowed her eyes and gave it a firm jerk. He snatched back.

"No, ma'am," Kayden reiterated, chin jutting. "Ain't had time to. Mr. Dominic took us out on the paddleboats before breakfast and showed us everything. They have a pool, and game room and—"

"Lots of horses," Jayden added, leaning against her hip. "They have lots of horses, Aunt Cissy."

"Uh-huh." Cissy relinquished her hold on the rope and nudged the bedroom door open with her heel. "Why don't you two go on in the room and wash up?"

"But Mr. Dominic said he'd let us pet the horses." Kayden frowned in concentration, winding the rope up in his fist. "He said they have painters and nickels."

Kayden whipped the rope out against the floor with a sharp snap, causing them all to jump.

"Easy, now." Dominic reached out, big palm up, for the rope. "And they're paint and quarter horses," he stressed with another dimpled grin.

"Yeah. That's what I said." Kayden's face puckered in affront but he handed over his prized possession with no resistance.

Cissy fought to keep her jaw from hanging open. Who would've thought this handsome, muscled flirt would be so good with kids? Most men only thought of kids as a nuisance. They dropped tail and ran at the sight of them.

Jayden squeezed her hand. "Mr. Dominic promised we could feed the horses."

"Regardless—" Cissy bent and steered the boys by their elbows through the door "—we all need to freshen up a bit. And I'm sure Mr. Dominic has other things to do."

Dominic cocked his head and shrugged. "Well, I did promise them. And I try not to break my promises."

His deep tone made her blood rush. It was husky and warm. The kind of voice a woman would expect a man to have first thing in the morning, his arms wrapped around her and his body hard.

Cissy firmed her mouth. *Promises.* She'd made one of those, too. And so far, she hadn't delivered. She had to get her feet back under her, regain her focus and avoid distractions. She averted her gaze from Dominic's knowing eyes.

All distractions.

"Yeah," Cissy muttered, "most men try not to break promises. But they're usually not successful."

Dominic's bright smile dimmed.

Cissy cringed at the bitter tone lacing her words. He'd been nothing but kind and she was being an ungrateful guest. Crystal would've kicked her square in the rump right about now.

She dragged a hand across the back of her neck and regrouped before speaking with more care. "That was nice of you to offer. But I'd hate to interrupt anyone's day."

"It's not an interruption." Dominic moved closer, bracing his hand on the door frame above her head. "I'll bring your bags up and tell Ms. Betty you'll be down soon. After you've had some breakfast, we'll head out. I'll show you around."

Cissy deliberately avoided the bulge of his biceps and focused on a point over his broad shoulder.

No distractions. If she had any sense about her, she'd turn him down flat.

But she couldn't disappoint the boys. It was rare for the three of them to be able to spend a day of leisure together. And lately, a day where she wasn't dragging them around in search of work from sunup to sundown.

"Okay." Cissy paused at the threshold. It was best to be straight with him from the get go. She clarified over her shoulder, "For the boys. I'd hate to disappoint them."

"I'll take it." Another grin crinkled the corners of his eyes and sparked a flirtatious glint in the dark pools.

She spun back around, placing the door between them with no finesse. Dominic's genteel tone and rugged charm were enough to reduce a woman to a puddle at his feet. And she refused to melt.

A quick shower, fresh set of clothes and pair of sneakers had her feeling halfway decent again. The boys showered next, taking full advantage of the toiletries provided in the en suite bathroom. Most of which ended up on the floor.

Mouth full of toothpaste, Cissy rubbed a towel over the boys' wet heads. Her cell phone vibrated with a clatter across the nightstand. She froze. It could only be Jason again.

"I can't breathe." Kayden's whine barely broke through the fluffy cloth of the towel draped over his face.

"Sorry," she muttered absently, slinging the towel away and rinsing her mouth in the sink. "You two finish up."

Unplugging her cell from the charger, she scrolled through and found over a dozen missed calls since last night. All of them from Jason.

Cissy shoved the cell in her pocket, her jaw clenching. That was it, then. She had to take his next call. If she didn't, she'd only make things worse. There was no way around it.

She helped the boys dress, then they made their way down to join Dominic. A large plate of pancakes, warm syrup and crisp bacon was waiting for her. Ms. Betty turned out to be a small, bubbly woman with a bright smile. And the boys weren't exaggerating. She had to be the best cook in Georgia. Kayden and Jayden even found room for second servings.

After waiting patiently for the boys to refill their bellies, Dominic led them outside and down a trail to the paddock. Cissy followed behind him and the boys, taking in the sights around her.

The bright morning sun hadn't quite begun blazing yet, making the air less humid. Several guests strolled about the grounds or splashed in a large pool on the side of the main building. Azaleas, grouped around the walkway, boasted brightly colored blooms.

Cissy inhaled, pulling in the sweet fragrance of the flowers and savoring the stroll down to a paddock below. The boys' giggles mingled with Dominic's deep tones, stretching a smile across her face. It was nice to ease her vigilant grip on them and relax.

She glanced around once more, noting the extensive grounds peppered with bunkhouses, roaming horses and guests enjoying outdoor activities of all kinds. Surely a bustling business like this would have a need for extra help.

Cissy smiled wider. A job. The first step of a solid plan to salvage the mess she'd made of her life. She'd ask if there were openings. Hopefully, there'd be something. If she could secure a job and board here, she could earn enough money to fix the car and save to pay for a new apartment. She'd work every hour of the day if she had to.

That was it. A strategy she could swing. A job, money and a new home.

She turned back and sighed with satisfaction at the boys' excited skips ahead of her. They bounced at Dominic's side with glee, stretching up every now and then to snag his jeans and tug for his attention. Each eager pull drew the denim tighter across his muscular thighs and buttocks.

Cissy's skin tingled. Dear Lord, that man had a fantastic a—

Stop. She had a plan now. Job, money, apartment. There was no room for diversions. And there sure as heck wasn't any room for a man. Even if he did have the sexiest butt on the planet.

Kayden released his hold on Dominic's jeans and tore off to clamber up a white fence surrounding the paddock. Jayden held Dominic's hand, pulling at it as he ran.

Dominic's attention clung to the lithe man who'd opened the door to them last night, who stood a few feet from them, grooming a horse. "I brought you some help, Logan."

Jayden added, "Mr. Dominic said we could pet the horses."

Logan's arm stilled, the brush hovering over the horse's back as he smiled at the boys. Tipping his hat, he stepped forward and held out his hand to Cissy. "Morning. Don't think we had a proper introduction last night. I'm Logan Slade. Dom's older brother."

She took his hand, his warm greeting putting her at ease. "Cissy Henley. I'm sorry about us barging in on you last night."

Logan waved away the apology. "Don't worry about it. I'm sorry I wasn't more cordial." His eyes cut to Dominic. "Just didn't know company was dropping by."

"Yeah, well, that'd be my fault." Dominic moved to the fence, lifting Jayden up on the rail beside Kayden. "Didn't think I needed to call seeing as how I'm family."

"You don't," an older man said, ambling up to the fence. "Both my sons can come and go as they please." He gripped Logan's shoulder, then stretched an arm out over the fence to shake Cissy's hand. "I'm Tate Slade. Dominic and Logan's dad. But you can call me Pop. Everyone else does," he added with a wink.

Cissy smiled, briefly shaking his hand and thanking him for allowing them to stay the night. He had a kind face and gentle voice. She could easily see where Dominic and Logan got their gentlemanly qualities.

Sidestepping the men, Cissy took up a piece of the fence, too. She lifted a foot and braced it on the lower rung. The rail's warmth seeped into her palms.

"Can we pet the horses?" Kayden asked.

He seemed fascinated by Logan's movements. His eyes clung to Logan's hand as it pulled a brush through the horse's hair with whispering sweeps.

"Sure." Pop retrieved an apple from a bucket. He handed it to Kayden and motioned toward a horse lingering nearby. "That one's named Oreo. Call him."

"Come on, Oreo," Kayden urged, holding out the red apple.

"Gentle," Dominic said. He lifted Kayden higher on the fence. "Stretch your arm out a bit farther. And hold your hand as flat as you can."

"What if he's not hungry?"

"Don't worry. Oreo never turns down a treat. He'll come when he's ready. You just have to be patient."

The large horse moved with ease toward Kayden's arm. Spots of midnight black and creamy white covered the horse's sleek muscles. Oreo dipped his broad head and nuzzled Kayden's hand with his nose, tugging on the apple with his teeth and chomping off a generous bite. Kayden dissolved into a fit of giggles.

"Oreo likes it," Jayden announced, promptly scooting closer to Dominic to lean over the fence, as well.

The boys' eyes sparkled and their faces flushed. Cissy smiled. She couldn't remember the last time she'd seen them this excited over anything. Of course, Crystal's illness had cast thick shadows over them for so long.

But watching them now, they seemed like their old selves for the first time in forever. Their laughter was genuine. Their comfort obvious.

Cissy closed her eyes and dropped her head back, enjoying the peaceful moment. The sun's heat poured into her muscles and her body relaxed on a deep exhale.

This was her promise to Crystal. Providing the boys with full bellies and the comfort of a permanent home. A life free of poverty and displacement. Something she and Crystal had never known growing up.

A buzzing in her pocket shot vibrations down her thigh. Cissy snatched the cell phone out, her fingers fumbling to keep it from falling to the ground. *Here we go.*

"Aunt Cissy, come look at this," Kayden called.

Pop had taken over with the boys and laughed with them as Oreo nuzzled their palms.

"In a minute," she hastened, shrugging as Dominic twisted to survey her. "I have to take this."

Spinning, she moved a few steps away and pressed the phone to her ear.

"Jason." It was impossible to drudge up a more polite greeting than that.

"Damn it, Cissy," he hissed. "Where the hell are you?"

She clenched her teeth and forced her voice to remain even. "Things weren't working out in Atlanta so I decided to move."

"The hell you say," Jason returned. "I stopped by the apartment yesterday. I know you got kicked out."

Cissy's temper rose, burning her face and neck. *Sleazy landlord.* No doubt, he'd been all too happy to fill Jason in with his version of the truth.

"Is that what that nasty piece of trash landlord told you?"

She grimaced as the words blurted out and glanced over her shoulder. The boys were focused on feeding the horse with Logan and Pop's assistance. Dominic, however, fully faced her. His arms crossed over his broad chest as he studied her.

Cissy tucked a strand of hair behind her ear and stepped farther away. "Look, I was behind on rent. I had it all worked out, but the landlord and I had a… disagreement."

Silence descended on the line. The soft push of a breeze was the only whisper on the phone for a few moments.

"Jason? Are you still there?"

"Yeah, I'm here." His voice softened. "A disagreement?"

"I handled it." She stomped on an anthill, watching a puff of dirt rise and the insects scramble.

"Yeah, you did," Jason stated matter-of-factly. "And then he evicted you."

"Look, I didn't have much of a say in the matter. I

made the only choice I could. And it was the best thing anyway."

"Are you okay? Are the boys okay?"

"They're fine." Her throat constricted, choking her next words. "What do you want, Jason?"

He sighed. "You knew this was coming. You can't keep running from it."

"I'm not running from anything. You and Crystal were the ones always skipping out. You'd show up out of nowhere, take her away for months at a time. Drop her back off then leave again." Her chin trembled. "You drove Crystal crazy, you know? Broke her heart a thousand times."

"Crystal understood. I never lied to her. She knew how important my career was to me. She knew I wasn't ready for anything permanent."

"Yeah? And what about the boys?" She lowered her voice. "Do you have any idea how confused they are about you? They don't even ask about you anymore. Jayden's too hurt and Kayden's too afraid of what the answer might be."

"Stop it." His voice cracked. "Crystal and I had this talk a long time ago. She knew I didn't want kids and it was her decision to go through with it anyway. I helped out when I could."

"How chivalrous of you," Cissy snapped.

"I loved her. You know I did."

She gripped the phone tighter. "Yeah. But not enough."

There was a scuffling against the phone. She could almost see him clenching his fists at his sides in angry frustration. Lord knew that was his usual posture when he was around her.

"I'm not going to fight with you, Cissy." Jason's tone tightened. "I'm calling because it's time. I got the adoption paperwork last week."

She froze. "No."

"It's the right thing to do."

"No. You're not doing this. Crystal left them to me. I promised her I'd keep them."

"I know this is hard for you. I know you love them." His voice shook. "In my own way, I love them, too. And this is the best thing we can do for them."

"It's the best thing for you, maybe." She shook her free hand violently in an attempt to fling off some of her anxiety. "It's not the best thing for them. I don't know how you can even suggest it."

"How can you suggest keeping them?" Jason shot back. "It won't be as easy to hold on to that pride of yours with two kids hanging on you. And you barely made ends meet before you had them, much less now."

"I'm working on that. I just need to get my feet under me and then we'll be fine. You won't have to lift a finger. Or a dime," she bit out.

"It's not just about the money. You oughta know that by now. Shit, Cissy. You and I would've made a lot more sense. Both of us loners. No ties, no obligations. Knowing our place and keeping it. You've always been realistic."

She froze, her heart slamming against her rib cage.

"We're not the type of people that get lucky in life," he continued. "And I'm not gonna gamble with my boys. You got nothing and nobody. That's just how it is. How it'll always be. There's no way this will end well," he scoffed. "Do you really expect it to?"

Cissy swallowed hard. The view before her began

to blur. The blue sky melted into the green fields. She snapped the phone shut.

There was nothing she could say.

DOMINIC STEPPED CLOSER and studied the tense line of Cissy's back. She remained motionless, the cell phone clamped by her side.

"Everything okay?"

Her head tilted. The silky strands of her hair slid back, revealing the jut of her chin.

"Yeah," she gritted.

"Doesn't seem like it."

He waited. The boys' laughter in the background rose. Snatches of chatter from guests strolling down nearby paths punctuated the stillness. But she didn't move or speak.

Damn sure wasn't anything worse than a stubborn woman.

Dominic shrugged. "Can't help if you don't let me."

Cissy jerked around, hands balled into fists. "Did I ask for your help? Did I ever once ask you for any help yesterday? Or today for that matter?"

His chest flooded with anger. Stubborn wasn't the word. Hardheaded woman wouldn't give an inch if her life depended on it.

"No. Can't say you did." He shoved his hands into his pockets and rocked back on his heels. "But all things considered, you should have. For those boys if nothing else."

The anger melted from her face and an embarrassed flush stamped her cheeks. She swung away and smoothed a hand over her hair before facing him again.

"Look, I…I'm sorry." Her throat moved on a hard

swallow. "Can I talk to you and Logan? In private?" She bit her lip, peering over his left shoulder. "Away from the boys?"

Dominic nodded, caving at the unexpected display of vulnerability. "I'll get 'em settled with Pop. He loves kids. He'll keep them busy."

Cissy dipped her head in response but maintained her silence. He pressed his lips together to keep from saying anything more. She wasn't skittish. But damned if she didn't keep throwing bricks on that mile-high wall she stacked around herself.

A small bundle hurled into Dominic's hip, jostling him. He looked down to find Kayden leaning against him. Jayden jumped down from the fence and rushed to Dominic's other side, weaving his fingers through his.

"Aunt Cissy missed the paddleboats this morning." Kayden grabbed Dominic's other hand and strained, trying to pull him forward. "So can we go again to show her?"

"Kayden, stop it." Cissy threw Dominic an apologetic glance.

Dominic stood firm and let him yank. The kid had a strong grip for such a small thing. He laughed when Kayden stopped tugging to let out an exhausted breath.

"Not right now, Kayden. There's plenty time for that. Your aunt and I need to talk."

"Can't me and Jayden just go by ourselves?" Kayden begged.

"No," Jayden said, his brow furrowed in concentration. "Mr. Dominic said we weren't to never, ever go in the water without an adult. Or a life per-suh-va."

"Preserver," Cissy corrected, waiting for him to repeat it. "That's good advice." She tossed Dominic a surprised glance. Her eyes warmed. "Thank you for watching out for them."

Dominic stilled. Such a different look from last night. Something pleasant streamed through his veins.

Pride.

It wasn't that he'd never felt proud before. It just usually only hit when he was standing apart from everyone. In the middle of an arena. Muscles tight, breathing hard and basking in his dominance over a thousand-pound bull.

It had always been a violent and overwhelming experience. But this was different.

Dominic focused on the snug grip of the boys' hands and the gratitude shining in Cissy's wide eyes. He wasn't alone. He was surrounded with warmth. With calm.

His chest rose. Supporting and protecting offered a new kind of pride. It was shared. It was quiet. But it was just as powerful.

"Well…" He cleared his throat. "Let me get them settled with Pop and we'll talk."

Dominic led the boys inside the paddock to drop them off with Pop and they were soon chattering a mile a minute as they were led from one horse to the next. Everything was new and exciting to them and Dominic caught himself missing the days he and Logan used to roam the ranch together as boys. He turned and walked back, reluctant to leave them but equally drawn to their stubborn, beautiful aunt.

"Mr. Dominic?"

He paused. Jayden had followed him a few steps and stood looking up at him with a grave expression.

"Are we gonna stay here for a while?"

Dominic hesitated. Damned if he knew why, but the boys' questions were intimidating. And he sure didn't know the answer to that one.

Jayden continued to study him and Dominic stifled the urge to toss out a flippant response. It was best to be honest.

"I don't know." Dominic tried for a comforting tone. "Don't worry about all that. Your aunt Cissy will handle things."

"Yeah, I guess," Jayden said. "But it's nice here."

Dominic took a moment to survey his surroundings through the boy's perspective. The green fields were wide enough to roll in for days. The soft sounds of the horses mingled with the distant laughter of guests enjoying the grounds. A warm breeze swept over his skin and ruffled his hair.

"Yeah," he returned. "It is."

Jayden smiled then darted back to join Kayden and the horses.

Dominic made his way back to Cissy, finding her deep in conversation with Logan by the fence. A spark of jealousy lit in his gut. It was unwelcome and unjustified. But it was there, all the same.

Whatever admiration Cissy held for him would pale in comparison to Logan's wealth of redeeming qualities. Logan was always the dependable, honorable son. Dominic had always been the reckless, carefree one. And Logan seemed determined to never let him forget it.

Dominic tightened his fists and his steps became purposeful. He'd forgotten why it wasn't always so nice here after all. Matter of fact, it was about time to hit the road again.

Cissy turned away from Logan and stilled when she

noticed Dominic. He slowed at her fierce expression. Her blue eyes were large and determined.

Tipping up her chin, she jerked her gaze away to focus over Dominic's left shoulder, studying the boys' antics in the field behind him. Not wanting to give her extra time to build a greater distance between them, he chose not to exit the paddock but walked up and faced her over the fence instead.

"So what's all this about?" Dominic asked.

She didn't respond at first. The skin of her hands paling even more and gleaming in the sunlight as she gripped the fence rail. Her knuckles began to whiten from the tight grip she had on the wood.

"My sister, Crystal, passed away a few months ago." Her throat moved on a hard swallow. "She had cancer. It was a really rough time for the boys."

Logan shifted at her side, ducking his head, his features firm. "We're sorry to hear that."

Cissy nodded and a muscle twitched beside her mouth. "Crystal left the boys to me. She asked me before…" She paused, squinting hard against the sun. "I promised her I'd take care of them. I've waitressed, cashiered and had just about every menial job you can think of so I'm no stranger to work. It's just—I've had a rough run of luck lately. The restaurant where I worked nights closed down and I had to quit my day job to take care of Crystal toward the en—" Her voice broke. "Anyway, I ended up losing my apartment. So I don't have a place for the boys at the moment. And I can't afford to get my car fixed."

Dominic felt a surge of admiration when she opened her eyes and looked at them both head-on.

"I promised Crystal I'd take care of them. And I

will," she said. "I just need a chance to get back on my feet."

"Well, we can always use another hand on the ranch," Logan said.

Cissy brightened. "That's what I was hoping—"

"It's hard work, though," Logan interrupted. He frowned, surveying her small frame. "Long hours. It can be rough."

She released the fence rail and turned to peer up at Logan. "I can do it. Whatever it takes. I've got to start somewhere soon. I have to. If I leave here now, the way things are, I know I won't have a chance. And if I lose those boys—" she inhaled deeply "—I'll lose everything."

Dominic's stomach dropped. If there was one thing Logan would understand, it would definitely be the loss of a child. Logan's features remained blank. Whatever emotion Logan felt, he kept it buried deep.

Dominic turned away. Why the hell had he waited so long to come home this time out?

"Please give me a shot," Cissy continued. "If I don't deliver, you can cut me loose."

Logan studied her for a moment, then sighed. "All right. First thing tomorrow, I'll show you around and get you started."

"Is there a chance I could start now? I can't pay you for the room last night or for our meals today. But there's enough hours left in the afternoon for me to get even if not ahead."

Dominic couldn't restrain the words bursting from his mouth. "Cissy, slow down. It's Sunday. Y'all just got what I imagine was your first good night of sleep in a while. Give the boys a chance to settle in and enjoy a couple days' rest with them first."

"No." She brushed him off, turning back to Logan.

Dominic was ready to fire back but Logan shot him a sharp look before saying, "Okay. But you'll need more space with the boys if you're gonna be here for a while. We'll go move your things to Dom's old rooms on the first floor. Then we'll get started. And I've got a friend that'll fix your car up at a decent price. I'll have it towed out to him."

"Thanks, Logan," she said, pumping his hand and smiling brightly before ducking under the fence and sprinting toward the boys.

"What the hell are you doing?" Dominic spat, glaring at Logan. "You gonna work her on a Sunday? She just pulled off the road."

"You heard her, Dom. It's what she wants to do."

"Yeah, I heard. But that's when you talk some sense into her and tell her to hold off for a few days." He watched her slow to a jog as she reached the boys. "Wouldn't it be better to let the boys settle in first before she hits the ground running?"

"Probably. But that's not what she wants, baby brother." Logan pushed off the fence and smirked. "And my advice would be to not try to talk her out of it. She doesn't seem to be the type to pander about."

Dominic sucked his teeth. That was for damn sure. But it was still worth a try.

His profile tingled under Logan's intense scrutiny.

"Easy, bro," Logan said, his voice firm. "You get tangled up in this and it'll trip you up when you get ready to hit the road again. Besides, you left me in charge of running the place. So it's not really up to you. That is, of course, unless you changed your mind and intend to stay put."

Dominic's shoulder tensed. He refused to face him.

"Yeah—" Logan's voice drifted off as he ducked under the fence and moved away "—that's about what I expected."

Dominic flinched. It wasn't so much Logan's words that wounded. It was the way he said them. The wry tone. As though there were no other possible outcome but for Dominic to disappear again.

He could hear him now. *Typical Dom. Give him an inch and he'll run ten miles.*

Though he couldn't blame Logan. He hadn't been much of a brother to him lately. Or at all, for that matter.

A crack of laughter rang out across the paddock.

Kayden straddled Pop's shoulders and whipped a lasso over his head. "Keep still, Jayden. I got it now," he called out, his voice faint but discernible.

Pissed though he was, that wrenched a chuckle from Dominic. Less than half an hour and that boy had his hands on another rope. Pop had probably handed his rope over to the boy as easily as Dominic had this morning. Pop always turned into a sucker when it came to kids.

The lasso whirled through the air and looped neatly around Jayden, who stood a few feet away, hands by his sides. Cissy unwound the lasso from Jayden. Kayden scrambled off Pop's shoulders, keeping hold of his end of the rope.

"Nicely done, Kayden," Cissy called. "Now give the rope back."

"Nope. Pop said I could have it."

"Kayden, you don't need it."

"Yes, I do."

"No, you don't."

"Yes, I do."

They struggled in a tug of war for a moment before Kayden snatched it from her grasp and tore off, a cloud of dust billowing with each step. Cissy took off after him, fussing the entire way. Pop and Logan laughed, Jayden bouncing with excitement between them.

Dominic found himself inching forward. Pop was in hog heaven with those boys. And Logan's laugh was the first genuine one he'd heard in ages.

Before he knew it, he was striding toward the laughter inside the paddock.

It'd be time to go soon enough. But right now, he was right where he wanted to be.

Chapter Four

"Gahlee! How much do these things poop?"

Cissy squinted tighter and squatted lower, scraping her shovel against the stall floor. The muscles in her shoulders and arms screamed with each forward thrust. The acrid smell of manure flooded her nostrils and billowed around her.

Wrinkling her nose, she wondered the same thing herself. Every afternoon for the past two weeks, they'd mucked the stalls. And every day it seemed to take longer and longer.

"Kayden, stop complaining and help your brother."

"But we've been doing this for forever," he whined. "I want to do something else."

Cissy drew upright, wincing at the ache that spread throughout her upper body, and prayed for patience. Kayden slumped against the wall, running that dang rope through his hands. Down, up and then back again. Just as he'd been doing for the past half hour.

She blinked away a fat drop of sweat that stung the corner of her eye and leveled a stern look on him. "I don't think you can really say you've been doing much of anything other than lollygagging and complaining.

If you pitched in and helped, the time would pass much faster."

"Yeah," Jayden piped from his crouch in the corner of the stall. "If you helped."

The shovel Jayden clung to extended several feet above him and the handle bopped against his head with each of his awkward movements. But he continued sifting through the shavings.

Kayden's face scrunched into a sour glare. "Who asked you?"

"I asked myself." Jayden glowered back.

"Cut it out, boys." Cissy gestured with a weak hand. "Kayden, bring the wheelbarrow closer." She smiled, giving Jayden a nod of encouragement. "Jayden, you're doing good. Keep it up."

Kayden groaned, then flounced out of the stall to stomp around the corner. Cissy rolled her eyes and firmed her grip around the rough handle of the shovel.

Stubborn whippersnapper. Everything always turned into a battle with him.

Kayden knew how to push her buttons better than anyone. No matter how hard she tried, she couldn't get a handle on that kid. The only one who seemed to have any control over him was Dominic. And darn if that wasn't a blow to her pride.

Cissy frowned. What was it Dominic had told her the other day? *Stick to your guns and don't give in.* She shook her head, slinging the sweaty strands of her hair away from her face. Easy for him to say. He just swooped in when it was playtime. He didn't spend every waking second with them, disciplining and correcting. Lecturing and worrying.

Worrying... Her worries had multiplied by a thousand since she'd taken Jason's most recent phone call.

She stabbed the shovel deep into the shavings. Jason knew where they were now. She hadn't been able to put off telling him anymore. He'd been strangely silent at the news. Then, he'd asked the question she'd been most afraid of.

Could he come down to meet her? They needed to talk.

She'd tap-danced around an answer but knew that wouldn't be the end of it. Jason was their father. And if she wanted a real shot at keeping the boys, she had to be smart in her dealings with him. Like it or not, one move from him could tumble her shack of cards.

"My arms are getting tired, Aunt Cissy." Jayden dropped his shovel and rubbed his hands up and down the outside of his arms.

"It's okay," she said. "Why don't you help Kayden with the wheelbarrow?"

He complied, taking slow, tired steps out of the stall to join Kayden.

Cissy cringed, dragging the toe of her shoe through the shavings on the floor. She had worked them hard the past couple of weeks. Maybe too hard. But she couldn't afford to pay anyone to watch them and, though they offered, she didn't want to take advantage of any of the Slade men's good nature. She didn't do charity.

"Okay. Here." Kayden rounded the corner and plopped the wheelbarrow down with a rocky thump. "Can me and Jayden go do something now? I bet Mr. Dominic would let us paddleboat again."

"No. You're not to interrupt the men during the workday. You know that."

He kicked the ground and slumped. "Well, can we at least take a break?"

"All right." Shavings sprayed as they took off. "But stay in the barn," she shouted at their backs.

"Okay, Aunt Cissy," Jayden whooped back.

Kayden, as anticipated, did not offer any promises.

Cissy waited until she heard their footsteps stop. The slap of the rope against the barn floor started up and their sporadic laughter chimed out. Relaxing, she turned back to her task.

Scoop, shake low and then tip out into the wheelbarrow. Repeat. Over and over. She plunged back into the job, sweat streaming down her nape and tickling her spine. She followed the barn manager's directions to the letter and angled each toss of the shavings so the smaller balls of manure would roll out separately.

Scoop, shake, tip, repeat. Again. And again. And again. Then move to the next stall.

A tired laugh burst out on her next exhale. Who would've thought she'd become such an expert on manure? She shrugged her shoulders with the last heave of the shovel. Who cared? As long as it brought in money. Her small pile had grown over the past few days, but she needed more. Every job counted.

"You making an art out of this or what?" Dominic's broad shoulders filled the entrance to the stall. His sexy rumble and come-hither stare commanded the small space.

Cissy's belly warmed. His T-shirt, snug as ever, clung to every bulge of muscle in his upper body. His long, thick legs were encased in denim and the ever-present buckle and boots just added to his appeal. He was the coolest, most intoxicating drink of water she'd seen in years.

And here she was. Sweaty, dirtied up and reeking of manure.

She lifted her chin. It didn't matter. There was no room for him in her life. Job, money and a new home. That was all she would think about.

"Someone has to do it," she returned. "It may as well be me."

His brown eyes skimmed down the length of her. "Yeah, but you could take a break once in a while. Let one of the hands help you out. You look just about dead on your feet."

Her lip curled. "Gee, thanks. What a charmer you are."

Dominic smiled, white teeth catching his lower lip, dimples popping. "I do my best, baby."

Sexy devil.

Dominic reached out, snagging the wheelbarrow with his large hand and rolling it closer to her. "Seriously, you need to take a day off. You've been working from sunup to sundown for two weeks straight."

"Yeah, well." She dumped the last wet clump of waste into the wheelbarrow. "I need the money."

"All you have to do is ask, you know? It's okay to ask for help every now and then."

She was sure her expression reflected her disdain.

Sighing, he shook his head. "Well, it's nice to see you took Pop up on his offer to watch the boys. That's something at least."

"What are you talking about?" She froze, tilting her head and straining to hear the slap of the rope again. "They weren't out there?"

"Out where?"

"Out in the barn," she stressed, pushing around him and dropping the shovel with a clatter. "I told them to stay put."

She scanned the entrance. No sign of them. Spinning, she darted back to the other end of the stalls, poking her head over the tops of each as she passed.

"Boys?" She hated the anxious tremble in her voice but she couldn't tamp down her worry.

"Relax, Cissy." Dominic caught her elbow, slowing her steps. "They're probably just out roaming around. Boys do that from time to time."

"I know that," she snapped. "That's the problem. There's no telling what they're up to."

"They're probably just out at the paddock helping Logan. It's time for the last trail ride to come in."

"No, they know they're not supposed to bother any of you when you're working."

Her mind raced to settle on the greatest likelihood of where they would go. Back to the main house? No. Ever since they'd arrived at the ranch the boys had wanted to stay outdoors.

Think, Cissy, think. What had Kayden been harping on lately? He hated work. Nothing new there. He wanted to tag along with Dominic. Well, Dominic was standing right in front of her and he wasn't with him.

She bit her lip. What had he asked about earlier? Paddleboats. But those always got anchored by six, and it was almost eight o'clock now. Surely they wouldn't try taking one of those out? There'd be no way they could get anywhere since the boats would be tied down.

Her blood rushed, pounding through her veins in

frantic bursts. There'd also be no one there to make sure they didn't attempt it. Or fall into the water trying...

"Kayden mentioned something about paddleboats earlier." The words broke past the lump in her throat.

Dominic's brow furrowed. His mouth opened but no sound emerged, a worried glint in his eyes.

That was enough to warrant her fears. She jerked out of his grasp and flew from the barn, her jeans pocket snagging on the handle of the wheelbarrow and tipping it over in the process.

"Cissy, wait."

Ignoring Dominic's call, she tore across the field back toward the paddleboat dock. It was fast approaching dark, making it difficult to discern more than just the outline of the boats in the distance.

Please let them be all right. Please.

"Kayden?" Cissy struggled to shout. Her chest burned. She panted and pushed forward, ignoring the shooting pains in her thighs. "Jayden?"

"Aunt Cissy!" Jayden's frightened voice drifted on the air whipping by her ears.

She reached the dock, her shoes pounding across the wood slats. Two yellow-and-white paddleboats were tied down on the right side of the dock. Her eyes fluttered shut as she sighed. They were still anchored.

She rushed to the other side of the dock, shoulders lowering at the sight of another anchored paddleboat. Then she saw a loose rope rising and falling with the swell of the water. Panic surged through her again.

Cupping her hands around her mouth, she shouted, "Jayden?"

"Over here." It was a breathless gasp.

Cissy ran around the dock house to the edge of the platform and peered across the pond.

Jayden's head bobbed above the water several feet out, his arms waving above him. "Kayden fell. Hurry."

She choked on a panicked sob and scanned the area around the paddleboat. Swift splashes broke out against the surface of the water. Kayden's drenched head appeared for a moment before it sank beneath the surface again.

Cissy plunged headfirst into the pond. She stabbed through the murky depths with her arms and legs, ignoring the sting of the water that splashed into her eyes. She couldn't afford to lose sight of them.

She reached Jayden first, gripping his arm tight and tugging him to the paddleboat bobbing nearby. A painful heave and he tumbled safely into it. She darted back through the water toward Kayden, his broken struggles becoming a dark waterlogged blur.

"Kayden…" His name spluttered out with a mouthful of water.

It became harder and harder to move. The heavy pull of her soaked jeans weighed her legs down, and her arms had about as much strength as jelly.

She kicked harder, crying out when her calf muscle cramped up. Instinctively, her body curled in on itself. Her hands wrapped around the lower half of her leg, and her head tipped back, leaving her to gasp for air.

"Ka—" The water rushed in, filling her ears and mouth. She spit it out, kicking her free leg to rise another inch out of the water. "Kayden…hold on…"

Kayden's splashes subsided. The surface of the water no longer sprayed with his movements. He was sinking. And she couldn't move.

"Aunt Cissy, help him," Jayden cried. He leaned over the edge of the paddleboat, his outstretched arm shaking.

"Kayd—"

"Help him," Jayden sobbed.

Cissy's chest tightened to the point she thought it'd rupture. Kayden was feet away and she couldn't move. *No, please, no...*

A loud splash sounded in the distance. Followed by another. She gulped in one last deep breath before the water rolled in over her face again, struggling with her free leg to kick back to the surface as the murky darkness swirled in.

The waistband of her jeans jerked back and up, digging into her belly. A firm grip yanked her to the surface before letting go.

"Get her in the boat," Dominic rasped, giving her bottom a hard shove before he turned and dived beneath the water.

A strong arm wrapped around her chest, underneath her arms, and pulled her backward.

"Breathe, Cissy," Logan instructed against her ear.

She craned her neck, straining to catch a glimpse of the stretch of water where Kayden had disappeared.

"Lie back." Logan's voice turned firm. His grip tightened when they reached the paddleboat where he lifted her arms up to the edge. "Can you pull yourself up?"

Cissy nodded shakily. Her throat burned. She wrapped her fingers around the edge and strained, Logan's hands lifting at her waist. Jayden's fingers dug into the collar of her T-shirt and pulled until she fell in a heap inside the paddleboat.

Jayden whimpered at her ear, tears pouring down his face. "I can't see him anymore," he whispered.

Cissy gulped in deep draws of air and pressed on Jayden's shoulders to lift her head and stare down at the dark depths.

Her stomach heaved. She couldn't see him, either.

DOMINIC THREW HIS arm out, grappling around underneath the water in a desperate attempt to locate Kayden. His lungs seized and sharp shards of pain shot through his chest.

He hung motionless as clumps of mud and algae danced around him. Kayden's small lungs would hold a lot less air than his. He kicked hard and dived deeper.

Come on, Kayden. Come on.

A wisp of clothing brushed his fingertips. He stabbed an arm out and managed to curl his fist into the boy's shirt. He tugged hard, bringing Kayden's body close and shooting to the surface.

Kayden choked and sputtered when they broke through to open air, fighting and succeeding in capturing much-needed oxygen.

Thank God. Dominic almost wept with relief.

Tremors racked the boy's frame.

"Easy, Kayden."

Dominic shifted, floating on his back and clutching Kayden to his midsection. He forced himself to loosen his tight grip.

Hardheaded kid. If Cissy hadn't thought to come looking for him here—

Cissy. His eyes shot to the paddleboat. She was safe inside, sagging with relief, arms wrapped around Jayden.

Kayden's second bout of coughing vibrated against his gut, commanding his attention and reminding him to get a move on. Dominic executed gentle kicks, being careful not to jostle the boy any more than necessary as they made their way to the edge of the pond.

He lifted Kayden out of the water and propped him on his side in the grass. The boy's slim arms and shoulders heaved in a quick rhythm on each cough and spit of dirty pond water before he became quiet and resumed normal breathing.

Dominic smoothed back the wet hair plastered over Kayden's eyes and cheeks, the buzzing in his blood making it difficult to maintain a steady hand.

Defiant, hardheaded kid. A minute or two more and Dominic would've been too late.

"Kayden, look at me." Struggling to keep the biting edge in his tone under control, he waited until Kayden lifted his head, the boy's blue eyes wide and fearful. "Do you have any idea how close you cut that?"

Kayden blinked several times, then nodded. "I'm sorry…" His chin trembled. "I didn't mean to—"

"Oh, you meant to all right." Dominic dug his hands underneath the boy's armpits and lifted him upright. "That paddleboat didn't untie itself. And what did I tell you about that?"

Kayden dropped his head, his words muffled against his soaked shirt. "Not to go by myself. And to always have a life per-suh…"

"Preserver," Dominic stressed. "If you'd had one of those on, you wouldn't be like you are now. And if you'd stayed put like your Aunt Cissy told you to, none of it would've happened to begin with."

Kayden wrapped his hands around Dominic's forearms and looked up at him, regret flooding his features. "I'm sorry," he whispered.

Dominic's anger fizzled, his heart melting.

Sweet, defiant, hardheaded kid. Who was he to judge anyway? His screw-ups had started long before he'd reached Kayden's age and hadn't stopped yet.

Sighing, he drew Kayden in and wrapped his arms around him, squeezing the solidness of his back and arms to assure himself that the boy was safe.

Jayden appeared, hovering at his elbow. Tears poured down his cheeks and dripped from his chin. "Is he okay?"

Dominic nodded, leaning back and releasing Kayden. The boys fell into each other's arms with slight sniffles.

The soggy slap of denim sounded. Cissy limped toward them, Logan close on her heels. Her face was drawn and her mouth tight. The honey-colored strands of her hair hung in soaked clumps.

She dropped to her knees beside the boys and tugged Kayden out of Jayden's embrace. Pinning him close, she held him for a brief moment before jerking him back and squeezing her hands around his upper arms.

"How could you do that?" Her voice rose. "I told you to stay in the barn. I told you."

Kayden's face crumpled. "I'm sorry, Aunt Cissy."

"No, you're not." She shook him, her pale arms and slight frame quaking. "You're not sorry. You're never sorry. You just run wild and do anything you want. You never listen to a word I say."

A pang of sympathy traveled through Dominic's chest. Fear had overtaken her. "Cissy—"

"How many times do I have to tell you to listen to

me?" The shaking turned fierce. "To just do what I ask?"

Her accusations became shrill. The tremors racking her small build grew more violent. Jayden sobbed heavily, his hands reaching out in an attempt to wrench her grip from his brother.

"You could have died," Cissy shouted, her voice hoarse. "And what about Jayden? He could've drowned as easy as you. You could both be at the bottom of that pond right now."

"But I'm okay, Aunt Cissy," Jayden pleaded, patting the soggy shirt plastered over her shoulders and trying to put himself between the two. "I'm okay," he choked out.

Dominic's heart constricted. He winced at the terrified looks on the boys' faces. As much as he understood her anger, it was hurting rather than helping.

"That's enough, Cissy." He reached out and pried her hands from Kayden, forcing her to rise.

"Let go of me." She shoved her shoulder into his chest and struggled to break free.

Her elbow caught his rib. Dominic pushed back, being careful not to hurt her with his tight hold.

"Stop it. You need to calm down. You're scaring them and you're gonna make yourself sick."

"Let me go!"

He met Logan's eyes over her head and jerked his chin in the direction of the boys, now wrapped around each other behind him on the ground. Logan nodded, moving past him.

"Calm down, Cissy," Dominic repeated gently, walking her backward. She stumbled several times, favoring her left leg. He stopped and smoothed his hands over her back, his fingers fumbling over the drenched folds of her T-shirt.

"L-let me g-go." She stammered the words over and over but her fingers clutched at him, pulling him to her.

At last, she grew silent. Tears wobbled on her dark lashes and her face contorted.

"It's okay," Dominic murmured, running a hand over her brow and pushing her wet bangs back. He stooped and scooped her up in his arms, carrying her over to one of the benches lining the pond.

She gasped when he set her down and braced her hands on the edge of the bench.

He apologized softly, running his palm down the back of her leg. "What's wrong here?"

"Ch-charley horse." Her teeth chattered. "I—I got it when I was in the water." She shuddered, her leg jerking beneath his fingers. "I w-was so c-close to him… but I couldn't…I couldn't—"

"Hey," he whispered. He looked up, squeezing her slim thigh and urging her to look down and meet his eyes. "Everything's okay."

Cissy nodded and dropped her head back against the wood bench. Dominic refocused on her calf, dragging the soaked leg of her jeans up to her knee. The muscle was tight. He wrapped his hand around it, rubbing the knot with the heel of his hand. She jumped and tried to pull away.

"Easy," he soothed. "I'm going to rub it out but you've got to relax. Otherwise, it won't work."

Her muscles drew tighter and her face clenched.

He had to distract her. She had her emotions bottled up to the point of bursting. If she didn't loosen up, she'd do some damage to herself.

Dominic conjured up a small smile. "You know, when I was a kid, I was just as bullheaded as Kayden. Logan was always the good boy. But I disobeyed every chance I got. Sneaked off on my own. And if I couldn't find trouble, I'd make some." He rubbed again, digging deep into the muscle. "It's a wonder I survived past ten. But I did."

The knot in her calf eased and her leg relaxed against his grip.

"What did your mom do?" she rasped.

An old, familiar memory flashed. The swirl of a white skirt and flip of a red handbag. A brush of lips on his cheek and a soft whisper—*Bye, Dominic.*

"Nothing." His stomach roiled. "She wasn't here for most of it. Left when I was eight…"

He paused in surprise, his words whispering off. As best he could remember, this was the first time he'd spoken of his mother to someone other than Logan. And that was rare at best. Their mother was a taboo subject at Raintree. One they all avoided at every opportunity.

It was too difficult a thing to revisit. Too hard to remember how easy it had been for his mother to smile, wave and walk away. Right into a waiting car and into a new life. Leaving all three Slade men standing in shocked silence in Raintree's dirt drive. Leaving Dominic to watch as she left without any of them. Without his shaken, grief-stricken Pop. Without grim, stoic-faced Logan. And without him, tears and all.

Because none of them were enough for her. And she hadn't needed them.

It hadn't taken long for Dominic to decide that he should leave at the first chance, too. That he had to get his own ride out of Raintree and stay the hell away.

Away from the memories of his mom not needing him. And from the knowledge he'd never be able to measure up to Logan's stringent model of what a man should be.

His palm still moved at Cissy's calf but no longer rubbed. It glided along her soft skin. He found the action comforting and it appeared to do the same for her.

"Not that it mattered when she left," he tacked on, swallowing hard. "If you trust Logan's take on it, she wasn't much of a mom anyway."

A soft cry brought his head up. Cissy's hands obscured her face and her shoulders shook.

Dominic rose swiftly and scooted in beside her on the bench. "Hey, come on now," he soothed, pulling her hands down and clasping them in his. "What's this?"

"What if I'm like that? What if I'm not much of a mom, either?" Her questions tumbled out in shaky bursts, jerking her small body. "What if I'm not fit to have them?"

"Okay, now, that's enough," he admonished, caressing the back of her neck with the pads of his fingers. "None of that is true."

"But—"

"But what? The only reason those boys are still breathing is because you had the instinct that told you something was wrong. And you were the only one that thought of looking for them at the pond." He smoothed his thumb over her cheek, brushing away a tear. "You know those boys like the back of your hand. And that doesn't come easy. It takes a lot of attention and a lot of hard work."

She examined his features. Almost as though she was trying to peer inside him and pick his thoughts apart. Her eyes moved beyond him. He followed her gaze to the field behind him where Logan's shadowy figure headed toward the house, Kayden in his arms and Jayden trailing behind.

"Dominic?" Her voice was soft and hesitant.

"Yeah?"

"I don't know what I'm doing," she whispered.

Warmth flooded his chest and spread through his body. How many times had he acknowledged that to himself over the years? Questioned his actions? His path in life?

Dominic shook his head and grinned, drifting the blunt tip of his finger over the delicate seam of her mouth. "Who does?"

She returned her attention to his face, her lips parting with a smile of her own. She moved into his arms, pressing her cheek to his chest and brushing her arms under his to cradle his back.

Dominic stilled. Something pleasant unfurled inside him and streamed through his veins.

He'd held a lot of women. Felt their soft curves against him. Excited them with his touch. But he couldn't remember a woman ever putting her hands on him for a reason other than sexual gratification. Or his wallet.

None of them had ever had such a gentle touch. And none of them had ever held him.

Breathing her in, he smoothed his hands over her hair. The strands, still wet, were straw-like and released whiffs of pond water and dirt. He nuzzled his face against it.

No cloying perfume or artificial pretense here. Just an honest, earthy bundle of woman.

He stayed silent for several minutes, savoring the experience and half afraid she'd bolt given the chance.

"I don't want to hear any more talk about you not being a good mom." He lifted her chin with his knuckle. "Matter of fact, it's only fit for one thing. And that's for tossing in that wheelbarrow of yours."

Cissy blinked, then closed her eyes in dismay, her shoulders drooping.

"What?" he asked.

"I just remembered." She gave a frustrated smile. "I knocked the wheelbarrow over on the way out of the stall. Every bit of what I cleaned up is probably all over the barn floor. It's going to take forever to get it all up."

He chuckled. "That's a perfect job for two disobedient boys. Especially since they put us knee-deep in it today."

She brightened, those blue eyes of hers beaming up at him through the darkening night surrounding them. Her small nose wrinkled, drawing focus to her sweet freckles. His arms moved of their own accord, drawing her close again to rest his chin on top of her head.

He realized he didn't know what he was doing right now, either. He'd never opened up this much to a woman. Had never taken a path as real and risky as this before. There was no telling where this was headed.

He ought to be careful. Wary, even. Cissy was just as unpredictable as any ride he'd ever taken in the arena. But as hard as he tried, he couldn't quite talk himself out of it.

Dominic grinned, pressing closer and absorbing her soft heat. *Well, hell*. He guessed he'd just have to see how long he could hold on.

Chapter Five

Cissy eased back in the rocking chair and inhaled. The air was moist and warm, filling her lungs and soothing her senses. It was early. Much earlier than the ranch guests usually rose and began milling about.

The sun was just beginning to peek above the horizon, the rays gentle. An early-morning dew sparkled on the grassy fields below. She closed her eyes and soaked it up, lifting her legs and rolling her feet in circles. The pain from last night had eased and her calf muscle had loosened up again.

"Here you go."

She rolled her head on the back of the chair and lifted her lids a bit to find Pop standing over her. A squat mug sat in each of his hands, steam curling from the rims.

"Thought you might like a cup of coffee," he said. "Didn't know how you took it so I just dropped a bit of cream and sugar in it."

Cissy sat up and smiled, taking one of the cups, cradling it and sipping slow. "Thanks. That's perfect," she murmured.

The chair next to her creaked. Pop settled his weight in it, leaned back and plopped his booted feet up on the white porch railing. He took a few sips of his own, then released a satisfied sigh.

"Crack of dawn's the only time during summer that you can really enjoy a hot cup of coffee and a good porch spell."

His silver hair took on an orange glow as the sun hit it. His lashes swooped down as he took another sip of coffee. The lines of his face eased and he moaned low in his throat. He opened his eyes and turned to her with a broad smile.

"Go ahead." He winked and gestured to her feet. "Throw those dogs on up there. If you're gonna do it, you might as well do it right."

Cissy laughed. She lifted her legs, one at a time, and tried dropping them on the porch rail. Only they wouldn't quite reach. Each foot fell short of the mark about four inches.

Pop guffawed. "I didn't quite take into account our difference in height, little bit. Scoot that chair on up there and show me how it's done."

She did as instructed, dragging the chair forward a few inches with her free hand then settling back down and throwing her legs up. Success!

"Good deal." Pop returned his attention to the view before them and continued nursing his coffee. "Where are the boys this morning?"

"Dominic took them out to the barn a while ago to muck some stalls."

Cissy grinned, recalling the boys' groans as Dominic had led them out of the room next to hers. Dominic's deep tenor had sounded outside her door, providing explanation that it was punishment for their antics the night before. Surprisingly, they'd accepted it with a minimum of resistance.

"Ah. It'll do 'em some good," Pop remarked. "Though I can't say I'm well versed in the art of discipline." He caught her questioning look and continued, "It's hard balancing protection and tough love when you're going at it on your own."

She nodded. "Was it difficult? You know… When you were on your own with Dominic and Logan?" Her face heated at his look of surprise. Maybe she was being rude for mentioning it. "I don't mean to pry," she hastened. "Dominic told me his mom left when he was young. I just wondered if it was as difficult for you with two boys as it's been for me."

He grunted. "*Difficult* ain't the word for it." His forehead wrinkled until he settled on the right one with a smirk. "Hellish, maybe. That would be a better description."

Silence descended for a few minutes, Pop gazing out at the fields and squinting his eyes against the rapid ascension of the sun.

"Logan was around ten when Julie left," he said. "Dominic had just turned eight. I was at my wit's end there for a while. What with dealing with my wife leaving, trying to juggle the ranch and chasing after them full time. I put a lot on Logan. Dominic, too, come to think of it." A gentle expression eased over his features. "But once we got our rhythm, there was no stopping us. We were a tiny unit but we were still a family. All three of us made mistakes. But we loved each other hard. Still do. And that's what got us through." He shifted, roving his gaze over her face. "Reminds me a lot of you and those boys of yours. The three of you against the world."

Cissy's cheeks warmed. She wanted to thank him for more than just the coffee. But she couldn't find the right words.

"Pop spouting tall tales again?"

Grass rustled against Dominic's boots as he and the boys approached the back porch steps. Jayden bounded up before him, his damp shoes pounding across the expanse of the porch. Kayden hung back, easing his way up behind the thick cover of Dominic's legs.

"I beg your pardon," Pop shot back with a sarcastic laugh. "I don't tell tall tales."

"Mmm-hmm." Dominic lingered at her side, tapping his blunt fingertips against her shoes propped on the rail. "You've got Cissy in story position. It was a fair assumption."

Dominic took his hat off, balanced it on the porch rail, then trailed his hand up to touch the back of her calf. A thrill shot through her. So did a fresh surge of embarrassment. She tucked her chin to her chest to hide the blush snaking down her neck.

Lord, she couldn't believe she'd blubbered all over him last night.

"How's the leg this morning?" he asked, cupping his warm palm against her skin.

"Better." Clearing her throat, she turned her attention to the boys. "Have you two been busy?"

Jayden nodded with pride, stretching across her lap to kiss her cheek. "We got up all the poop, and Mr. Dominic said we did so good that if you were feeling better, we could go fishing."

"Oh, yeah?" She squinted up at him. She was sure he would've had his fill of them after last night.

Dominic's dark waves moved with his nod, falling

over his tanned forehead. "Yep. Thought it was about time y'all had a day off. And it's a proved fact that fish bite better on Sundays."

"That all depends on the skill of the fisherman," Pop inserted.

"Are you a good fisherman, Pop?" Jayden sprung to Pop's chair, ducking beneath his propped legs and wedging in between.

"The absolute best, my boy." Pop dropped his feet from the rail, set his coffee on the porch and swept Jayden up in his arms.

"Do you think I could be a good one?" Jayden asked, smoothing his fingers over the stubble lining Pop's jaw.

"Hmm, let me see those hands." Pop took Jayden's hands in his and turned them over. His brow wrinkled and he put on a grave expression as he examined the palms. "Looks as if you got all the hallmarks of a fine fisherman. Can't say you'd have any trouble."

Jayden scrambled higher in Pop's arms and issued a theatrical whisper in his ear. "Will you come with us and show me your skills? I want to catch more than Kayden."

Pop chuckled. "I think I will join y'all. But what you say we work together on this? If I taught you and Kayden the same things, we might catch enough fish to fry up tonight. Whatcha think, Kayden?"

Kayden edged around Dominic's thigh and nodded. "Yes, sir."

Cissy took stock of him. He shifted his weight from foot to foot, fists shoved deep in his pockets, and hovered off to the side. Very meek and reserved. Very un-Kayden-like.

"Kayden?" Dominic ruffled his hair, squeezing him

to his side for a second then nudging him with a knuckle in Cissy's direction. "Why don't you show your aunt Cissy where the tackle is and gather it up while Jayden and I get some bait together?"

Dominic bent, divested Cissy of her cup and wrapped his hand around hers to pull her up. Her skin tingled under his touch. The warmth radiating from his long, muscular length beckoned and she fought the urge to lean into him.

"Sounds good," Cissy said. She brushed past Dominic and made her way to Kayden, taking his hand in hers.

"You remember where I showed you in the shed, Kayden?" Dominic asked.

"Yes, sir." Kayden squeezed Cissy's hand tight, tugging to lead the way down the steps and back across the grass toward the barn.

The farther they drifted away from the porch, the quieter it became. The only sounds were the dewy grass sweeping against their legs and the soft chirps of crickets. Kayden's grip remained snug.

Cissy glanced down at him as they crossed the field. He held his head high and took confident steps but kept parting his lips only to think better of it and look away again.

She bit her lip to keep from prodding the thoughts out of him. It was best to wait and let him share when he was ready. Otherwise, he'd clam up and hide away whatever was bothering him even more than before.

"Aunt Cissy?"

"Yeah?"

"I am sorry, you know?" Kayden halted, pulling her to a stop. "I really am."

Cissy knelt, ignoring the wet grass on her bare legs. She took his face in her hands and smoothed a strand of blond hair off his forehead.

"I know." She sighed, rubbing her thumbs over his soft cheeks. "I'm sorry, too. I shouldn't have lost my temper but you disobeyed me. And, more than that, you scared me, Kayden."

He dropped his head and twisted the toe of his shoe in the grass. "I didn't mean to scare you."

"I know that, too." She tipped his chin up and he cocked his head, bringing his eyes to hers. "But I was scared just the same."

"I won't do it again. I promise."

"I hope not. I'd be lost without you and Jayden. I don't know what I'd do if anything happened to either of you. We're a team, you know?"

A broad smile burst across his face. He hurled himself against her, knocking her to the ground. Laughter bubbled up from her belly and she relaxed into his embrace, rocking him from side to side on her back.

"I love you, Aunt Cissy," he whispered, planting his face against her neck and tightening his arms around her.

Her breath caught, her heart full to bursting. She hadn't really gotten it before. But she did now.

This was really the promise Crystal had begged for. This was what she had wanted for the boys. Something all the money in the world couldn't buy.

And it was the only thing that really mattered.

"I love you, too, Kayden."

He slid off to the side, plopping onto his back and tucking his hands beneath his head. "You think Mama's up there?"

Cissy tilted her head back and looked up. The sky was clear and blue. Not a single cloud to be found. The sun had fully risen and lent a gentle morning heat to the air around them. Just the kind of day Crystal had loved the most.

"I know she is."

"Do you miss her?"

Her throat tightened and she turned her face away, concentrating on the tickle of the grass pressed against her cheek. "Every day."

"Aunt Cissy?"

She swallowed hard and blinked several times before turning back to face him. "Hmm?"

"What's it like to have a grandpa?"

"I don't know. Your mom and I never had one."

He frowned, pursing his lips. "You think grandpas go fishin'?"

She smiled. "I suppose."

He nodded. "I think Pop would be a good grandpa."

"I think you might be right."

"I bet he'd show me how to catch more fish than Jayden." He sprang up and bent down to yank her to her feet.

"Pop said he'd show both of you, Kayden," she reminded. "So don't go monopolizing his time, okay? And how about we not make today a competition? How about we just enjoy our time together?"

Kayden frowned, squinting his eyes and opening his mouth with a disgusted expression.

Cissy placed her hands on her hips and hid her grin. "Let me put it this way. If you don't play nice and do as you're told, you'll be shoveling poop every morning for the rest of the week."

He closed his mouth and lost the attitude.

She couldn't resist bending down to kiss his cheek. He scrunched his nose, dragged the back of his hand over his face then took off.

"Wait for me, Kayden," she called, her words bouncing off his back as he tore toward the shed behind the barn. She laughed. He was such a rubber ball of trouble.

"I gotta get the tackle," he hollered over his shoulder. "Mr. Dominic and Pop are pro'ly ready to go."

Cissy sobered, her steps slowing.

Dominic.

If Kayden was beginning to imagine Pop as a grandpa, what thoughts could he be entertaining about Dominic? The boys spent an enormous amount of time with him despite the heavy workload she gave them. And they were still young enough to want to latch on to anyone within three feet.

But Dominic wasn't just another guy. He was turning out to be different somehow. Patient. Calm. Protective. And understanding. A combination of traits she'd never expected to encounter all at once in a man.

Cissy rubbed her hands up and down her bare arms, trembling despite the warm summer sun. She'd never felt as safe or as comforted as she had last night in Dominic's supportive hold.

She stilled. Maybe Kayden was on to something. Maybe this ranch was more than just a pit stop. There might be more here than she anticipated.

And that was what scared her the most.

She couldn't afford to make a mistake. And Dominic could very well end up being the worst one of all.

DOMINIC DIDN'T KNOW when he'd had such fun fishing. It was one thing to sit motionless in a boat and wait in silence. It was another thing altogether to step up to the edge of a pond and toss a line out with twin boys full of energy.

Especially a pair that could talk the hind leg off a mule.

"Dang it," Jayden cried, yanking his rod back.

"Jayden, watch your language." Cissy cast a stern look at him, then resumed her relaxed stance with her fishing pole.

Her ivory cheeks were flushed with sunburn and her freckles had multiplied by a cute dozen. They'd been out for several hours now. The abundance of the day's catch and sustained enjoyment of everyone had kept them at it longer than he'd intended.

"That worm jump off your hook again, Jayden?" Pop called out. He stood several feet away, recasting his line.

"Yeah," Jayden grumbled, lifting the rod higher and dragging the empty line up on the bank.

Dominic squatted at Jayden's side and rustled around in the grass to find the empty hook. He held it up between his thumb and forefinger. Using his free hand, he sifted through damp soil piled in a disposable foam cup to snag the tail end of a worm seeking escape.

"You got to wrap it around the hook, buddy," he instructed. "Sometimes it takes a few sticks."

Dominic held the frantic worm up, smiling when Jayden threw a hand up over his eyes. There wasn't an inch of space between his fingers.

"Ew. Its guts go everywhere."

"Sometimes. But it's a means to an end." Dominic waited for him to uncover his eyes. "See, you stick it once—"

"Yuck."

"Then wrap it, stick it again…" Dominic paused to gain better control over the flailing end of the worm and pulled it snug. "And stick it one more time so it's all bundled up tight on the end of the hook."

"Gag a maggot! I ain't doin' that," Jayden wailed before darting behind Cissy's legs and burying his face in the back of her thigh.

Dominic rolled his lips together and forced his breath out of his nose. He didn't want to laugh out loud. It'd damage the boy's confidence.

"I hate to break it to you, Jayden," he said. "But if you don't stab that sucker good, it's gonna fly off every time you toss that line out."

"Dominic." Cissy's tone and frown were serious but her mouth twitched. She reached up to swat a gnat. A big flake of damp dirt flew off her fingertip and landed on her chin. Both her hands were caked black with soil and worm waste.

Dominic grinned. No worries there. Cissy had no problems sacrificing a worm for the sake of the catch.

He rose and tipped his head down to Jayden, putting on the face he reserved for solemn occasions. "I'm sorry, Jayden. It's just a fact that you have to get acquainted with worm guts to catch a fish."

"What about a plastic one? Can't he just use that?" Cissy reached back and smoothed her wrist over Jayden's head, keeping her soiled fingers away from his hair.

"If we were fishing for trout, yeah. But we're snagging bream. And they go after live bait."

Kayden made his way over from Pop's side and held his hand out to Jayden. "Come on. Pop said we need to start cleaning the fish if we want to have 'em cooked for supper."

Pop waved from his position, where he was already gathering up his tackle, and called out, "We've been out here awhile. 'Bout time to get these fish ready for frying. I'll take the boys on up and we'll get started cleaning 'em."

"But I don't wanna go yet," Jayden complained. "I ain't got but a few."

Kayden snagged his brother's hand and jerked. "Come on. My bucket's full. You can have some of mine."

Cissy's eyebrows rose and those deep blue eyes widened to almost twice their size. Kayden noticed, too. He twisted his chin over his shoulder and smirked.

"Yep. Just playin' nice like you told me to, Aunt Cissy."

The words were almost sung. Kayden flashed Dominic a look as the two moved off, scrunching one side of his face into an oversize wink.

Dominic choked on his laughter and winked back. That kid was too smart for his own good.

"Don't encourage him," Cissy advised, poking a dirty finger in Dominic's chest. She still held her "I mean business" tone but her own giggle destroyed the effect.

Jayden sprang back, barreling into Dominic's leg and tugged on his T-shirt. Dominic knelt down once more, bringing his face level to Jayden's.

"Thanks for takin' us fishin', Mr. Dominic." Jayden's whisper tickled his ear with each rushed word. "I don't like the worms but I like the fish. And I'll do better next time."

Jayden swung his head to the side and smacked a kiss on Dominic's cheek, then threw his arms around his neck and squeezed.

Dominic pulled him close and ruffled a hand through his soft hair before saying, "You can't get any better, buddy. You're already the best fishing partner a man could have."

That new pride was back. It swelled in Dominic's chest and flooded his body. He had one more second to treasure it before Jayden slipped free to join his brother. The pair scrambled off, fishing rods clanging, to join Pop on the trek back up to the house.

Dominic rubbed a hand over the base of his throat. He could still recall Jayden's insistent tug on his neck the first night they'd arrived. His whispered plea for Dominic to still be there when he woke up.

At the time, he'd shied away from it. Didn't feel he deserved that much trust or admiration given his reckless past and bad record of dependability. And, Lord knew, he wasn't built to be anyone's hero.

But that was then. He stood taller now. Stood prouder. Now he cherished every wistful glance and tender hug the boys gave him. He felt new and rebranded. As if he'd earned a second glance.

Maybe even a third...

"You're good with them."

Cissy's soft murmur brought his attention to her. She was eyeing him again. Roving those beautiful blues over him and peering deep. He shifted from one foot to the other.

Damn, he'd give every dime he had if it'd buy him a way inside that guarded mind of hers. Give him a glimpse of what she was thinking. What she thought of him. But he didn't want to run her off. Or have her lock him out again.

Instead, he acknowledged a simple fact. "Because of them. They're easy to love."

Cissy pinched her lips together and her face flared an even deeper shade of red before she looked away. The words seemed to disappoint her. She stepped closer to the edge off the pond, reeled in her line and picked off the remnants of a soggy worm.

"Their mom was like that." Her brow furrowed as she tugged on the wet line to secure the hook. Fingers shaking, she used a lot more time and focus than needed to complete the task.

"Crystal?" he asked.

"Yeah." She turned and bent to lay the fishing pole on the grass. "People were always drawn to my sister. I'm not sure if it was the same for our mom or not. We never got a chance to know her."

"What happened to your mom?"

"She got pregnant with us before she got out of high school then passed away when we were born. Our aunt took us in. She and my cousin were all there was left of our family." She stood, rubbing at the mud on her hands. "Crystal and I spent the first six years of our life dirt poor and crammed in a trailer with our aunt and cousin." She sighed. "After a while I think it just got to be too much for my aunt. Twins aren't really two for the price and time of one." Her laugh was humorless. "She gave us up for adoption. Crystal and I stayed in foster homes until we aged out of the system." She shrugged. "When I got evicted from my apartment, I tried to contact my aunt. Turns out she died a few years ago," she said softly.

She put her back to him, looking out over the pond. Focused on something he couldn't see.

"Crystal and I knew our aunt had been in a tough position. We understood why she thought she had to give us up. And we knew she loved us." Her voice lowered to a whisper. "But, sometimes, it just seemed as if she didn't love us enough. As if no one did. As though we weren't worth the trouble."

Dominic took a few steps toward her before forcing himself to stop. Hell, he knew exactly how that felt. Not being needed. Or wanted. He ached to reach out and wrap his hands around her upper arms and pull her against him. Urge her to lean into him. Make her feel his strength at her back and know she wasn't alone.

But his mind balked at shattering the moment. He locked his knees and waited.

"Crystal and I were each other's home." Cissy glanced at him over her shoulder and tried for a small smile. "We never felt alone as long as we had each other. And we were identical, just like the boys. No matter how many strangers surrounded me, I could always look at her and feel like I belonged."

Her mouth twisted. "Crystal never had trouble trusting people like I did. Especially men. That's how she ended up with Kayden and Jayden. She fell for this random musician and ate up every lie he fed her." She frowned and shook her head. "No, that's not fair. Jason didn't always lie to her. As a matter of fact, he was pretty blunt on a lot of occasions. I guess she just heard what she wanted to hear."

No longer able to restrain himself, Dominic crossed the last bit of distance between them, removing his hat and dropping it on the ground next to her fishing pole.

He took her hands, turning them over a time or two and rubbing his thumbs over the thick dirt covering them. Giving them a gentle tug, he brought her to a sitting position beside him on the ground close to the edge of the pond. He dipped her right hand in the cool water, rubbing at her delicate fingertips to dislodge the dirt from them.

"Do the boys ever see him?" he asked. He didn't know how many answers he'd get, but he was willing to push for as many as possible.

"They used to. Every now and then for the first few years. Jason would come around to see Crystal and he'd spend some time with them. But then he and Crystal would always take off and I'd stay with the boys until she got back. It'd usually be a month or two. About as long as he had off between gigs at the time."

"How 'bout since then?" Reaching down, he pulled his shirt from his waistband and wrapped her wet hand in it to rub it dry.

"Once or twice. When Crystal got sick, he came around more often to see her. By then, the boys didn't really know him. They just knew *of* him."

She studied his movements. Followed his hands as they returned to the water to begin cleaning her other palm.

"Was that him on the phone that day? When you first got here?"

"You remember that?" She seemed genuinely surprised.

"Yeah." How could he forget? That one call had altered her entire demeanor. Made her spine rigid and brought tears to her eyes.

Her lips parted a couple times but no sound emerged. She swallowed hard then everything came rushing out.

"He wants me to give them up. He says they'll be better off with two parents and a nice suburban home." Disdain dripped from her words. "He says he loves them even if he doesn't want them. And that I'm being selfish for trying to keep them."

Dominic lifted her hand from the water and wrapped it in his shirt, repeating his motions from before.

"Crystal and I weren't lucky like others," she said. "We never got adopted or had a stable home. People were always coming and going out of our lives. I don't want that for the boys. And I promised Crystal I'd give them more than that."

She ran her tongue over her lips in a nervous gesture. "Jason thinks I have nothing to offer them." She hesitated. "Do you think he's right?"

"Hell, no." Dominic's answer was immediate. It burst from his lips on a spurt of anger.

The bastard. How blind could a man be? How could he not see how important Cissy was to those boys? What she brought to them?

He wrung his shirt around her hand with more force than necessary, wiping firmly at her skin and dragging every mark off her.

"Dominic, don't. You're ruining your shirt." She issued a halfhearted smile and tried to pull her hand away. "I'm filthy."

He shook his head. He released her hands and lifted his palms, smoothing off the fleck of dirt from her chin and cradling her flushed cheeks. Emotions he'd never felt before washed over him, leaving him weak and wanting.

"I've never met a woman more pure and sweet than you."

Her rosebud mouth parted on a swift intake of air and he moved in, nudging her lips with his. He waited, giving her a chance to respond before asking for more. Every muscle in his body strained against his rigid hold.

To his relief, she met him halfway, pressing her soft mouth to his and trembling in his arms.

It was all he needed to let go.

His tongue swept between her lips, dipping inside and gathering the taste of her.

Sweet. Intoxicating.

He had to have more. Plunging deeper, he moved his hands into her hair, rubbing the silky, blond strands between his fingers. Her light, sweet scent drifted around him and he fell even deeper into the kiss. Into her.

A soft sound escaped her mouth and entered his own. He reluctantly drew back, pressing his forehead to hers and closing his eyes. She bunched her hands in his shirt and tugged him closer.

"Dominic…"

A question? A plea? Quiet cry of surprise?

He wasn't sure. But damned if her soft sigh and the sweet taste of her on his tongue didn't make him weak and desperate. Weak for more and desperate to hold on.

"Yeah?" he asked, speech slurred and husky.

At her silence, he opened his eyes and leaned back to find her studying him. Only this time, her gaze wasn't as focused. It was dazed and excited.

Her hands uncurled, leaving his shirt, smoothing up his chest and wrapping around his nape. Tingles spread over his scalp and down his spine when her fingers combed through his hair. The corners of her mouth tipped up, her expression shy.

Her big blue eyes wandered over his face and lingered on his mouth.

"Will you do that again?" she whispered.

Dominic's heart tripped in his chest. *Would he do it again?*

If he did, he'd fall so fast there wasn't a chance in hell he'd be able to avoid the impact. But if he walked away, he'd never know how deep this feeling ran.

And he'd never know how far she'd let him in.

"Yeah," he murmured, touching his mouth to hers. "As much as you want."

Chapter Six

"One more, girl, and that's it."

Cissy jumped, her head smacking into the underside of a picnic table and her fingers fumbling over the red ribbon wrapped around them. She eased back on her heels and looked up with a laugh.

A young woman stretched over the edge of the wide wood table to peer down at her with raised brows. "Did you hear me? Just one more table to decorate and everything'll be set."

Tammy Jenkins. She'd arrived at Raintree Ranch a couple of days ago with her cousin, Colt Mead, to celebrate Independence Day. They were both taking a short sabbatical, as they put it, from the rodeo circuit to enjoy the holiday. And they were both close friends of Dominic.

Dominic...

Cissy sighed. It'd be exactly a week tomorrow since their fishing trip. If she was being altogether honest about it, she could probably cite the number of minutes that had passed from the exact second his lips had touched hers. Her mind had wandered back time and time again to his kiss by the pond, leaving no room for any other thoughts.

Despite his strength, he'd been nothing but tender. Warmth pooled low in her belly at the remembered feel of his mouth on hers. His big, warm palms kneading her nape. His deep, sexy rumble a soft whisper over her skin.

As much as you want...

"Sorry," Tammy said. "Didn't mean to break your concentration."

Cissy blinked, realizing she was staring blankly at the disarrayed bundle of material in her hands. Tammy's fingers curled over hers, gathering up the wayward ribbon and bundling it back into the bow she'd been tacking to the smooth wood of the picnic table.

Cissy shook her head and smiled. "You didn't. I was just thinking about..."

About... She scrambled to try to find a reasonable excuse for where her mind had been. *Dominic.*

No. The party.

His mouth...

No. The horses.

His touch...

No—

"You're busted, girl." Tammy grinned wide, brown hair streaming over her shoulders as she rose. She studied her through narrowed eyes. "I know exactly what you were thinking."

Cissy bit her lip. The heat from the scorching July sun was no match for the embarrassment that blazed through her body. She opened her mouth but couldn't manage a sound, her useless jaw hanging.

"You were thinking about how nice it is to have a night off from those wild nephews of yours." Tammy propped her hands on her hips, green eyes sparkling.

"You'll be able to relax. Dance. And maybe even enjoy an adult beverage or two."

Or find a dark corner and ask Dominic to kiss her again. Cissy clenched her teeth at the sudden thought.

Or ask him to touch her. Or ask to touch hi—

Stop it. Stay focused. She shouldn't have given in to begin with.

Cissy squared her shoulders and nodded. "You're right. That's exactly what I was thinking."

Tammy winked. "Can't blame you. I mean, I fell in love with those two on sight, but good golly, Miss Molly! Those two spitfires could burn the world down with a wet match if they set their minds to it."

"Who y'all talking about? The twins?" Jen Taylor, Tammy's friend and fellow barrel racer, arrived, plopping a basket full of condiments on the ground by the picnic table.

"How'd you guess?" Tammy asked, sharing a laugh with Cissy.

Cissy used the edge of the table to pull herself to her feet and eyed the decorative bow for any adjustments. The annual Fourth of July celebration at Raintree Ranch would kick off in just a couple of hours. She'd spent the better part of the day setting up with the staff and a few guest volunteers while the boys trailed after the Slade men.

It had been hard work but seemed like more of a treat. It'd been forever since she'd been able to socialize with other women her age. In the past, she'd spent the majority of her time with Crystal and the boys. And when Crystal became sick, her time had been split between hospital trips, work and worry. There'd been no time for fun. Or for herself.

And the cherry on top of it all was the fact that the boys would be spending the night out camping with the other kids as part of their Fourth of July treat. Pop and Logan would be leading the excursion, leaving her free of worry and able to enjoy the night's festivities. If Tammy and Jen's tales regarding past Raintree celebrations were even half-true, the night promised to be more than just festive.

"Where are the little toots anyway?" Jen lifted a hand to her brow, nudging a red curl back and shielding her brown eyes from the harsh afternoon sun.

Cissy motioned across the wide expanse of the field, focused on constructing one more bow from the last of the red ribbon. "They're over there helping the guys set up the portable stage for the band." Her laughter traveled down her arms and shook the ribbon in her hands. "Or, at least, they're over there anyway."

"Well, I hope they've been drinking that bottled water we left out for them." Jen fanned her neck, her nose wrinkling. "It's hot as Hades out here."

"And speaking of hot," Tammy whispered.

Cissy glanced up from her handiwork and followed the women's gazes through the hazy air to find Dominic, Logan and Colt making their way over to the picnic tables. The three ambled across the high grass, shirts saturated with sweat and clinging to their chests. Jeans tight and pulling in all the right places.

It was a sight no fully bred Southern woman could resist.

"Mmm, mmm, *mmm.*" Jen's fanning turned furious. "Maybe this *is* Hades. Because those have got to be the three hottest devils in Georgia."

"Two," Tammy said. "Colt doesn't count."

"Why not?"

Tammy's mouth stretched on slow, exaggerated syllables. "Because he's my cousin."

"So? Doesn't mean I can't have a gander." Jen eyed her from the side and shimmied her chest suggestively.

"Ugh, Jen." Tammy rolled her eyes. "You're ruining the moment for me. And don't let Colt hear you say that. His head's big enough as it is."

"Don't worry." Jen smoothed a hand over her fiery hair, her expression sly. "I know how to handle Colt."

Tammy's groan was long suffering.

Cissy ducked her head and laughed. Today was definitely more of a treat than work. Though she couldn't say she hadn't enjoyed the past few days of ranch labor.

She admired Dominic's long stride, recalling how his jeans had stretched over the thick muscle of his thighs when he'd squatted at her elbow to repair a fence earlier that morning. Since their fishing trip, he'd jumped into the daily fray of chores. Most often the ones near her or at her side. And afterward, he always made it a point to find an evening activity they could enjoy with the boys. She'd begun anticipating those two late-afternoon hours with Dominic as much as Kayden and Jayden.

Still, Cissy made certain their frolicking didn't interfere with work. She'd clocked in six days this week and had managed to pay off the dab of engine work and two of the new tires her car had required to be put back in working order. Only two tires left to pay for and she'd owe nothing more to Logan's mechanic friend. She'd be free and clear of debt, allowing the small stash of money she'd earned to flourish faster.

But she'd learned not to sacrifice too much of the time she spent with Kayden and Jayden, planning to reserve one day every week just for them. And it was an added bonus that Dominic seemed to enjoy being around them. Because she'd found herself growing more and more eager for his company.

"Hey, ladies." The trio had arrived, and Colt leaned on the picnic table with big hands, trailing his gaze from the top of Jen's head to the tips of her turquoise boots. "Gotta say, makes a man's work a lot easier having such pretty scenery on the job."

"Really?" Jen mocked with a bewildered tone. "What was it that struck your fancy? The cow patties or the horses' behinds?"

Colt grinned, running the tip of his tongue over his lower lip. "I don't know. It was a tough call." He smirked when she turned and bent over to retrieve the basket she'd stowed by the picnic table. "Though I'm rather partial to behinds."

Dominic chuckled and slapped a hand on his friend's back. "Ease up, man. You're getting into dangerous territory." He turned to Cissy and winked.

"Nah." Colt pushed away from the table and jerked his chin. "Jen and I have an understanding."

"Yeah," Jen chirped, rising and looking at Dominic. "I understand Colt's hit his head one time too many falling off bulls. So he suffers from delusions. Like the one where all women adore him. I just don't pay him any attention."

"Baby, you can't help *but* pay me attention," Colt defended, rubbing a hand over his broad chest.

They all laughed as the two sparred. Dominic drew closer, curling a hand around Cissy's hip.

Cissy stood taller and ignored the heat of his touch. *Focus on work.*

The stubble on his jaw brushed her temple…

No distract—

…right before his sensuous mouth touched her ear.

"Have to agree with Colt," he murmured. "Work does go a lot faster with you around."

She closed her eyes and a soft sound of appreciation escaped her. It was impossible to concentrate on anything other than the warmth of his big palm on her and the spicy scent of him surrounding her.

She cleared her throat, taking a step back and angling away to the last picnic table. She focused on centering the bow just right before tacking it to the wood corner and saying, "Well, I think we've all accomplished a lot."

"Too right, girl," Tammy added. "And it's getting close to party time. You boys wanna join us for a pre-party drink?"

"Sorry, no can do, ladies." Colt dragged a hand through his blond hair and tugged at his soggy shirt. "Gotta wash the stink off me so I'll be presentable for tonight."

"How gallant of you," Jen observed, lips twitching.

"Don't worry, baby," Colt murmured with a sexy wink, "I'll be sure to save a dance for you."

Jen smiled wide. "You hope you'll be that lucky, cowboy."

Tammy looked at Logan. "What about you? Ever since we got here, you've done nothing but work. Care for a drink with old friends?"

Logan tipped his hat, tossing Tammy a quick glance. "Thanks, I appreciate the offer. But I've got to make the rounds and make sure everything's in place for tonight."

He turned, taking long strides back to the main house.

Jen whispered out of the side of her mouth, "That is one heartbroken man."

"I know," Tammy said quietly. "He's been through a lot. Hasn't been the same since his wife left. Just wish there was something we could do to cheer him up."

Colt issued a sound of disgust. "Why don't y'all stay out of that man's business?" He cocked his head at Dominic. "*Women.* I'm gettin' the hell outta here before they start in on mine."

"Oh, we don't have to work hard for that, Colt, seeing as how anything with two legs and a bosom is your business." Jen teased at his retreating back. "How 'bout you, Dom? You playing tonight or what?"

A muscle in Dominic's jaw jumped. He glanced away, shifting his weight from foot to foot. A deep flush of red swept up his neck.

Cissy's stomach dropped. She busied herself with unnecessary adjustments to the bow she'd tacked up.

"No thanks, Jen," Dominic answered. "I need to get cleaned up a bit, too."

Dominic's boots appeared beside Cissy's sneakers. She hesitated before glancing up, striving for a blank expression.

"We left the boys with Pop," he said. "I'll send them to your room later. I know they'll want to say goodbye before they set off for camp." He leaned down, brushing a kiss across the bridge of her nose. "Think about going in soon. You're getting sunburned."

"All right." Cissy shrugged, trying for nonchalance but failing miserably.

Dominic's dimples broke out. "Save me a dance, okay?" He tipped his Stetson before walking away, his broad shoulders and slim hips an achingly impressive sight.

Dancing. When was the last time she'd danced?

Cissy nibbled on her nails, freezing when she caught Tammy and Jen staring openmouthed. "What?" she asked.

Tammy recovered first, her voice soft. "Are you thinking of playing tonight, Cissy?"

Cissy resumed gnawing her nails, wincing when she hit the quick. Was she seriously entertaining the idea of cutting loose with Dominic?

No distractions. That aggravating voice in her head returned and she knew she should listen. It was a bad idea. She couldn't possibly—

But did she want to? *Heck, yes.* The answer reverberated in her head, drowning out all other thoughts.

Tammy's hand touched her elbow. "You're entitled to some fun, Cissy."

"Yeah," Cissy said. She lifted her chin and firmed her features. "Yeah, I am."

"Well—" Jen adopted a mischievous expression "—what did you plan on wearing tonight? Because I have a little blue number that will knock Dom's socks off."

Little was right. An hour later, Cissy stood in front of the dresser mirror in her room, pulling at the hem of the sundress Jen had loaned her and barely managing to make it reach midthigh. Cissy shuddered to think of where it fell on Jen. The other woman had to be at least three inches taller than she was.

She scooped up the half-empty wineglass off the dresser and took a deep swig. Shaking her arms out to release some nervous tension, she glanced over her shoulder at her reflection. This was definitely a new look for her. Much more risqué than she was used to.

Still, with dressy cowgirl boots and a bit of makeup, it looked respectable enough. Though if the boys were going with her, she'd have opted for jeans and a T-shirt. That would've been much more suitable.

But the boys weren't going to be there. She had the evening to herself. To do with as she pleased. One night of fun. One night to let go. That was all. Just one night.

She twirled once, the skirt fluttering around her upper thighs. She took another sip of wine, and the sight of her blue fingernail polish against the glass made her laugh. Jen had assured her the shade was in and perfectly acceptable for women their age.

Their age. The two women were twenty-two. Only three years younger than her. But next to them, she felt ancient. Cissy frowned and smoothed a trembling hand over her hair. Then added a fresh coat of lipstick.

She'd had relationships in the past. Very short, very casual ones. Before Crystal had had the boys. But even then she'd shied away from anything serious. And serious was definitely a risk she couldn't afford now. Every choice she made affected Kayden and Jayden.

Only, Dominic was different from the other men she'd dated. Or any she'd ever met before. He seemed honest and straightforward. Safe, even.

"Just one night," she stated to the familiar stranger in the mirror.

Just one night. She'd ask Dominic for one night and get him out of her system.

"Aunt Cissy."

She started at Jayden's call, the wineglass tipping in

her hand. She sat it back down, out of sight, and stepped over to the boys hovering in the doorway.

"Hey, you two. Ready for a big night of camping?" Squatting, she threw her arms out and smiled. Her arms grew heavy when they both hung back, surveying her with quizzical expressions.

Jayden moved into her arms with slow steps. He pulled back to run his fingers over her dangling earrings, another loan from Jen, and frowned. "You look like Mama. When she used to…"

Cissy froze. She had no trouble finishing the sentence.

When she used to go away with Daddy.

Jayden's hands played at her ears for a few moments then dropped to encircle her shoulders. He pressed his face into her hair, breathing deep before murmuring an approval.

"She still smells like Aunt Cissy," he tossed over his shoulder to Kayden.

Kayden remained in the doorway, examining her from head to toe.

"Kayden?" Cissy shifted Jayden to the side. "Can I have a hug before you take off?"

He tilted his head to the side, not quite meeting her eyes, then shuffled over.

Drawing them in close, she kissed the top of their blond heads. "I'm going to miss you two tonight."

"Will you?" Kayden interrogated with harsh tones.

Cissy eased back and tapped Kayden's chin until he raised his head.

"Yes. Very much." She held his stare.

"Come on, Kayden." Jayden gave his brother a tug, then darted toward the door. "Pop said to hurry."

Kayden moved out of her embrace and joined his brother. He paused on the threshold and turned to face her. "You're staying here tonight, right? You're not going anywhere?"

Cissy shook her head for emphasis. "I'm not going anywhere. I'm staying right here. And I'll be waiting for you when you get back tomorrow." She used her most teasing tone. "You better take notes on this trip. Because I'm going to quiz you on the do's and don'ts of camping when you get back."

Kayden's scowl melted away under a prideful grin. "I'll be ready."

He took off, his feet pounding down the stairs.

Cissy rose and returned to the dresser. Snatching up the wineglass, she tossed the remainder of the wine back in one gulp. She swallowed hard, forcing down the bittersweet vintage.

Just one night. Get him out of your system.

Cissy put the empty wineglass down gingerly. She tugged at her skirt. One distraction was okay as long as there was a time limit on it. This one had to expire as soon as the sun rose.

She straightened the lipstick tube on the dresser, carefully avoiding her reflection, then made her way to the door.

"Just one night," she whispered.

DRINKS FLOWED. MUSIC POUNDED. And you couldn't take a step without nudging your neighbor. For Raintree Ranch, this was a rare occasion. For those in the rodeo circuit, it could easily be referred to as…last night.

Dominic tightened his grip around the neck of the beer in his hand. The chilled bottle had warmed long ago and the soggy label kept clinging to his palm. Any other time, he'd be on his third or fourth by now. And any other time, he'd be getting a kick out of Colt's rambling drunken chatter.

But for some reason, neither of those things did it for him tonight.

"And you know Ol' Boy is a big boy, yeah?" Colt's voice sounded at his side. "I mean you saw that sucker take a nosedive out of the chute the last time we…"

Dominic sighed, his gaze straying from Colt back to the crowded field before him. The Fourth of July celebration was in high gear. He had to hand it to Logan. He sure knew how to throw a party and turn a dollar at the same time.

Midnight was right around the corner, and the mob of people dancing in the floodlit field seemed to swell instead of dwindle. Dominic visually sifted through the crowd, straining to catch the flash of a blue dress. Every now and then, it'd peek out from between the crush of bodies. He'd keep an eye on it for as long as he could then it'd disappear again.

And he'd have to start all over.

Colt's voice rang in his ear. "That side-winding son o' a bitch jumped…"

There it was again. That slip of blue cotton.

The front line of bodies stomped then spun, giving him a full-on view of Cissy. She laughed, swaying with the crowd. Her blond hair bounced, then swung with her turn. That short skirt of hers did the same thing. The damn thing crept farther and farther up the slim curves of her ivory legs. Dominic's body tightened. He'd never loved or hated a skirt so much.

"...whole lot of 'em ran around like a bunch of nin-nies on a..."

Her boots slipped on the grass and the guy beside her took her elbow, steadying her.

Dominic's fist clenched. *Sleazy bastard.* That cowboy had been trailing her for the past hour.

Cissy flashed a smile. Just a polite smile. Then nudged the cowboy off.

Dominic grinned, his hand uncurling. *Atta girl.*

The crowd shifted again, blocking his view. Dominic stretched his neck to the side and strained to track her down again.

"And you know what that fool said?"

Fingers wrapped around Dominic's forearm and gave it a good shaking. Beer sloshed out of his bottle and splashed onto his boots. Colt fell into Dominic's side, grinning and shouting over the band's music at their backs.

"That fool said, 'You got a light?'" Colt paused, shoving his face closer. "Can you believe that? *You got a light?*"

Colt's deep laughter got the best of him. It rattled his frame, causing him to stumble and tip his own beer.

Dominic grimaced. There went another hefty splash against his boots.

"I swear, that had to be the funniest shit I've ever heard," Colt whooped, throwing an arm over his belly and shaking his head.

"Sorry." Dominic threw a hand up to his ear. "I didn't catch all of it."

Colt regained control of himself and adopted a somber expression. "What's up with you, man? You ain't listened to a word I've said all night."

"I don't know. Just not feelin' it tonight, I guess." Dominic shrugged, then turned back to the crowd.

There she was. The song ended and Cissy spun once more to a smiling stop. She clapped with everyone else, looking up at the band, cheeks flushed and breathing hard.

"Uh-huh." Colt's tone tamed. "I get it."

"Get what?" Dominic tore his eyes from Cissy and faced Colt with what he hoped was a bland expression.

"Hey, cowboys," a feminine voice chimed.

The brunette bumping her way in between Dominic and Colt with her hip was anything but bland. Painted face and tight jeans, she'd taken the same path to them that three others had over the course of the night.

"Mind if I join you?" she asked, eyeing Colt. "Makes a girl feel special being surrounded by such strong, sexy men." She pressed against Dominic's side and fluttered her lashes up at him. "Dom, right?" Her pink nails tugged at his platinum buckle. "The Dom Slade? PBR World Champion?"

Dom. As if she knew him. As if she knew he'd welcome her touch. He brushed her grip aside and moved his beer into his other hand. He was unable to escape her eyes, though. They clung to every inch of him, invading and stifling.

The woman's bravado slipped at his silence. She tossed her hair over her shoulders, casting nervous glances into the crowd.

"I had a bet going with my friends that you were him." She giggled. "I'm just about sure of it. So are you?"

Dominic met Colt's eyes over her shoulder. Colt

cocked an eyebrow and shrugged, turning away to take a deep swig of beer.

Dominic relented with a grumble. "I'm Dominic Slade, yeah."

"Well, Dom, I was wondering…"

There it was again. *That damned nickname.* An endearment on his friends' or family's tongues. But a curse on a stranger's.

An almost breathless Cissy jogged up to his side. Her short blond hair fell around her flushed face in shiny disarray.

"Dominic?" She held out a hand, palm up, and rushed out, "Would you like to cash in on our dance now?"

She smiled but her hand trembled and her expression was unsure. It cost her. He could see that at once. He'd rectify that right away.

"I'd love to." Dominic moved to take her hand but his forgotten beer intruded.

"I'll get that," Cissy said.

She grabbed the bottle and moved to toss it in a nearby waste barrel. Pausing—apparently thinking better of it—she upended it and took a deep swig before trashing it with a clang.

After taking his hand, she stopped and mumbled, "Dutch courage. Just so you know, I don't do this very often."

Damn, this little beauty meant business. She tugged him forward, weaving between couples swaying to a slow country beat, then turned to move into his arms.

Dominic's tension eased and he pulled her close. She laid her cheek on his chest, and he took a moment just to savor the soft curves of her body against the hard line of his. They swayed in unison, pressing tighter together with each brush from a neighboring couple.

"You don't need Dutch courage with me." Dominic's voice emerged with a husk. He cleared his throat. "I thought you knew that."

"Maybe not with you," she murmured, her words slow and slurred. "But you weren't exactly on your own, in case you didn't notice."

The sour note in her voice didn't escape his attention. He rolled his lips, trying to keep his smile from spreading.

"So you saw that, huh?" He tilted his head to sneak a peek at her face but she just snuggled closer. Her hair tickled his nose, forcing his grin to grow. Unable to resist, he pressed a soft kiss to the top of her blond head. "Well, consider us even. I spent the better part of the evening watching that cowboy follow you all over the damn field."

She lifted her head, her brows drawing down. "Who?" Her expression quickly turned mocking. "This is a ranch, Dominic. There's nothing but cowboys out here."

Laughter escaped him. "Nevertheless, I noticed one in particular that took a shine to you."

"I hope so," she returned softly.

He stilled. Those big beautiful blues were on him again. Easing right through his skin, deep inside. They gazed up at him, soft and undemanding. Adoring, almost. So different from any other woman's.

A heavy weight unfolded in his gut and seeped into his veins. Whom did she see? Dom, the champion bull rider full of good times? Or Dominic, the sometimes dependable guy who came through in a pinch?

And, more daunting still, could he live up to either?

"What do you see?" Dominic winced, his face flaming. The words had tumbled out before he could stop them.

"What?" Confusion clouded her delicate features.

It was too late to back out now. And he'd be damned if he did.

"When you look at me," he urged. "What do you see?"

Cissy remained silent, studying him again. Then she slid her hands up to caress his chest.

"A good man," she stated, her voice just carrying over the swell of the music.

His stomach dropped. He jerked his head to the side to hide his expression.

A good man. Those were a dime a dozen. One on every corner. Nothing special. And everyone knew they always finished last with nothing to show for it.

"Is that all?" He closed his eyes at the bitterness in his words.

The gentle warmth of her palm touched his jaw, nudging his face back to hers. He opened his eyes to find her rising on her toes. Her words soft and sweet in his ear.

"When you've never known one," she whispered, "it's everything."

Something strong enveloped him. It surged outward from his chest and blazed through his body. Every inch of his skin tingled, dancing as though life had just been breathed into it. It was overwhelming.

"Dominic?"

Trembling, his hands moved of their own accord to

grip her upper arms and press into the soft flesh. He fought like hell to keep from crushing her against him.

"Will you come up with me?" she asked.

She tugged his shirt, motioning to the path leading away from the rowdy clamor littering the field. Toward the main house.

He swallowed hard. "Yeah."

At that moment, he'd follow her straight to hell if that was where she wanted to lead him.

It took her several minutes to navigate a path through the clutter of dancers. He took over when she faltered behind a clump of ranch hands moving with chaotic jerks to the tune of liquor and laughter. Dominic swept her under his arm, holding her tight to his side, and plunged ahead.

"Wait." Cissy laughed once they cleared the chaos and emerged onto the dirt trail. "I just need to get my feet under me."

Her voice was giddy. Dominic stopped to steady her, tracing the blushing curve of her cheek with the pads of his fingers. He was such an ass. Dragging her across the ground with force. Ten of her steps to two of his. He'd probably scared her. Given her second thoughts.

He rolled his shoulders and dropped his head back. Away from the lights on the field, the stars were bright, blinking at him. A soft summer breeze lifted the night heat from his face and drifted down his neck.

"Okay," she said, taking over again.

She wrapped her small hand around his and led the way up to the main house. Inside. And to the door of her room.

Cissy pulled him in, then reached around to nudge the door closed. Dominic dropped against it, the hard wood pressing into his back and Cissy's soft curves caressing his front.

She nipped and teased his throat. The tip of her tongue traced over his skin, shooting zips of electricity up his spine. He snatched in some air before swooping down to catch her mouth. He plundered it, thrusting inside.

The sweetness of her filled his senses. He moaned, angling deeper with a hand against her head when the subtle hint of beer—*or was it wine?*—hit his tongue. With reluctance, he pulled back and glanced down at her.

Her face was flushed, her breathing labored. And she wobbled a bit on her toes. He wasn't sure if it was drink or nerves that caused it. But he knew she'd had her fair share of both tonight.

A good man. That was what she'd said. He was a good man.

His groan of frustration was audible. What would a good man do right now? Take advantage of her moment of weakness? Give in to the demands of his body even if she might be at a disadvantage?

His body locked down with defiance at the thought of walking away. His mind raced to find a justification to continue. Maybe she wasn't at a disadvantage. Maybe she did still have some control.

"Cissy? Is this really what you want?" She didn't answer. Only sighed and leaned in closer. "Look at me."

Shifting, he slipped his leg between her knees and nudged her up against him. She gasped, her body tumbling to the side before she caught herself, hands at his chest, and righted on her own. The warm, damp core of her settled over the hard muscle of his thigh.

Dominic's breath left him on a rush. It was exquisite torture.

"Please."

Her soft plea whispered over his skin before she took his mouth. She recaptured control, undulating against him and overpowering what little sense he had left.

She was warm. And soft. *So damn soft...*

He tipped his head down, realizing his hands had found her breasts. His palms cupped them, lifting them with gentle touches, relishing their weight and feel. His thumbs drifted over the hardened peaks, the thin material of her dress just a flimsy barrier.

She damn near purred. Heaven help him. *It wasn't enough*. He wanted more.

Moaning, he moved his mouth over them, laving and suckling, ignoring the cling of the cloth.

"Please. Just—"

Her whimper of pleasure spurred him on and led his hands down her back to knead the smooth curves of her bottom. *More*. He drew her hips up his thigh to meet the hard demand of his. Then slid them back down again. Pulling stronger with his hands and mouth. Over and over.

"Please," she begged again, winding her arms tight around him. "Just one night."

A heavy discomfort intruded. Dominic raised his head from her breast and blinked, trying to fight off his unease. He tried to concentrate on the soothing pass of her fingers through his hair.

It didn't work.

"Cissy, hold on." He tried to shake off the unease. Tried to focus.

She pulled and pushed at him with equal force. It

didn't make sense. Something was wrong. He examined her face and tried to pin it down.

But he'd grown too hard. His thinking was too blurred. He struggled to keep his hands on her arms, away from the parts of her he wanted to hold the most. Something clawed at the edge of his mind. Something strong and unpleasant.

"Just one night," she whispered, eyes closed.

That ominous shadow tore into his gut, leaving him winded. He scrambled to put a name to it. To what he was feeling…

Was it fear? Anger?

Betrayal.

"Stop." He winced at the accusing grate of his voice. He firmed his grip, stilling her arms at her sides.

It was all too familiar. The taste of alcohol lingering in his mouth. The rush of blood and excitement. The shared knowledge of a few hours of pleasure.

Just one night. Those hellish words returned. Words that had no place on Cissy's tongue. Haunting and shaming.

Just one night. Like so many empty ones before it.

A sudden urge to smother his face with his hands ripped through his chest. He tensed, tremors tearing through him at his restraint.

"You d-don't want…"

Her eyes were open now. Her soft stammer highlighting the hurt and embarrassment in the blue depths.

The tide of anger left him on a frustrated sigh. It wasn't her fault. None of it was. It was no one's but his own.

He cupped her face with shaky fingers, kissing her forehead before lowering his against it. She couldn't be more wrong. He wanted. Knew with terrifying exactness what he wanted.

"Oh, I want, Cissy." He inhaled, forging ahead before he lost his nerve. "There's nothing I want more than to be inside you."

She balled her hands into fists against his chest. "Then, why—"

"I want inside here." He touched his thumb to her temple.

At her silence, he dropped his hand and placed it over the upper swell of her breast.

"And I want inside here." He hardened to the point of pain at the rapid pound of her heart. Easing her from him, he lowered her feet to the floor and moved her back. "I can't manage that in one night."

She shifted from one foot to the other, face flaming. Her hands moved to her dress, pulling up the neckline and tugging down the skirt. The material at her breasts clung, still damp from his mouth.

His body screamed. *Damn.* He wanted to mark her more than that. Wanted to brand her. Needed to make it known she belonged to him.

He jerked his restless step toward her to a halt.

There she stood. Wringing her hands in her dress in much the same way she had her first night here. Except it had been Kayden and Jayden that had marked her then. Left a visible imprint from when they'd slept at her breast, waiting for a room.

Yearning bloomed in his chest. Those boys had a right to her. She devoted herself to them. And they lived each day without any doubts that tomorrow held the same promise. He wanted that same assurance. And so much more.

"I want it all, Cissy," he said. "I want everything."

Dominic froze. The excited heat searing through his veins iced into blocks. Hell if he knew where the thought had come from. Or how it'd escaped him.

His palm lifted, fingers reaching into the empty air as if to draw the words back. As if to catch them, wad them up and rub them out.

"But what if I can't give you that?"

Cissy's hesitant question trembled. She tucked a strand of blond hair behind her ear. Her blue eyes widened, lush mouth quivering. The fear on her face increased his.

Curling his hand into a fist, he dropped it to his side and shook his head. *What if he couldn't give it to her, either?* At a loss—*at a complete damned loss*—he left the room, shutting the door firmly behind him.

Chapter Seven

The morning after. Was that what they called it?

Cissy closed her eyes and rubbed the heel of her hand into her forehead, trying to ease the relentless throb residing there. It only served to heighten the waves of nausea rolling through her belly. She pushed the plate of bacon and eggs farther away with a finger.

Two feminine moans of sympathy sounded softly from across the table.

"Oh, gosh, girl. You look bad."

"How long has it been since you had a night of drinking?"

Cissy peeled one eye open to find Tammy and Jen leaning across the kitchen table, their faces wreathed with worry.

"A while," Cissy whispered.

Years, in fact. And it would be another long set of them before she tried it again. If ever.

"Well, at least it was for a good cause," Jen said. "I mean, you had a worthy goal."

"A delicious, sexy goal," Tammy added with a wink and nudge.

A laugh bubbled up before Cissy could stop it, her shoulders and stomach jerking with it. Her head pounded harder and saliva flooded her mouth. She held up a shaky hand.

"Please don't," she begged, softening the request with a hand on Tammy's arm.

"Sorry," Tammy whispered through a pained grin.

Tammy and Jen returned to their breakfast, gobbling it up with delicate gusto. Cissy pulled a hot mug of black coffee closer and took a sip. There were small blessings, at least. One, the coffee. Two, the ranch hands and guests had lived it up for much longer than she'd anticipated, sleeping in and leaving the grounds almost empty. Three, it was quiet.

Cissy sighed. Though she wasn't sure if that was a blessing or more of a curse. When it was quiet, she had time to think. To remember. And the last thing she wanted to do was dwell on her behavior at last night's shindig.

She stifled a groan. She must have looked like a fool to Dominic. She'd stalked him for a dance, dragged him up to her room and attempted to jump his bones. No wonder he'd put the brakes on.

But he hadn't. Or, not all together. He'd just turned the tables on her, his words shocking her.

I want it all, Cissy. I want everything.

For a moment, the painful pounding in her head faded. Her stomach turned over but for a different reason. Warmth pooled low in her belly and her heart raced.

Dominic wanted everything. He hadn't implied it. He'd straight-up announced it with conviction. And she'd loved him all the more for it—

Wait. The relentless throbbing returned and her stomach churned on a fresh wave of nausea. *Loved?*

Where had that come from? She'd known her attraction to Dominic had steadily grown but she hadn't anticipated it morphing into something so much stronger. Something so unpredictable and uncontrollable. She'd always been so careful. So aware.

She froze. Did he suspect? Or had he already known? Was that why he'd been so determined last night?

"You sure you're okay, Cissy?" Jen eyed her.

She sat up straighter and fiddled with the napkin in her lap. Then reached for the most convenient excuse.

"Right as rain. Just tired is all. I didn't think the boys would be coming back so early."

The boys. Her mouth ran dry. For a moment, she'd forgotten.

Her cell phone clattering across the nightstand an hour earlier was what had dragged her hungover butt out of bed. Logan had explained the boys were anxious to get back and had asked to come in ahead of the others. They were packing up and would be returning soon.

Longing streamed through her veins. Even though her night had been full, she'd missed them just as much. It was odd sleeping without them next door. Not hearing their late-night giggles and soft snores. Already, she was looking forward to holding them close and hearing the thousands of tales they'd have to tell from their camping trip.

"I don't know how you do it." Jen paused, crunching off a bite of bacon. "Taking care of those boys day in, day out. Barely having a moment's peace."

Cissy smiled despite the painful hangover. "It's kind of nice, actually. Once you get used to it."

And it was. Kayden and Jayden had become the center of her world. They stretched her limits and made her stronger. Commanded her devotion and taught her how to love. How important it was to love.

So, why shouldn't she love Dominic?

No distr— No damn reminders were needed! She shushed the aggravating voice in her head. This thing with Dominic was far beyond anything that could be termed a distraction. It'd turned out to be so much more. And, whether he knew it or not, Dominic did have a hold on her heart. Which was disconcerting because there were two small pairs of hands already clutching it.

"Well, I see the women are up bright and early." Colt's cheery drawl boomed across the kitchen, reverberating in Cissy's ears.

"Bring it down a little, Colt," Tammy said. "Some of us aren't used to late nights like you." She nodded in Cissy's direction.

Big, warm hands settled on Cissy's shoulders from behind. Fingers caressed them before drifting up to gently massage her neck.

"You okay?" Dominic's deep tenor vibrated at her back.

Cissy's head tilted forward, her throat moving on a hum of pleasure. Unable to speak, she nodded.

Dominic moved away to plunder in a couple of cabinets, his shirt stretching across the broad muscles of his back. A bottle rattled and glass clinked before he moved to the sink. He ran the tap, then retraced his steps to the table, placing two pills and a glass of water in front of her.

"Try to get that down. It'll help." He waited for her to comply, then continued as she swallowed. "Logan just pulled up with the boys. They're unloading their gear into the shed now. Should be up in a minute."

"Okay." Her stomach rumbled. She took another sip of water.

"I can take them for a while if you need a few more minutes." Dominic's handsome face creased with concern.

She shook her head. "No. I'll be fine."

He nodded, hesitating by her chair for a minute. "Colt and I mucked the stalls already. I'm about to hit the paddock and saddle up some horses for the first trail ride. I figure Logan's had a long night and could use the help."

Cissy winced good-naturedly. "I'm sure he could. He sounded tired on the phone. The boys probably put him through the wringer. And that's not counting what he had to go through with all the other kids."

"Well, I've got him covered. And you've earned a day, so just hang here and spend it with the boys." He dropped a kiss on the top of her head. "Get some rest."

"I thought we were hittin' up some training today?" Colt wedged a chair in between Tammy and Jen and began polishing off their breakfast remnants.

Dominic's smile was small. "Maybe tomorrow. Got stuff to do today."

"Damn, man." Colt frowned. "You been off the circuit for a while, and from what I've heard, you haven't laid eyes on a bull in over a month." He flung out his hands. "Nothing against that. I'm taking a break, too. But you still got to train. And I could really use some pointers."

"Tomorrow." Dominic turned and left, tossing over his shoulder, "Promise."

Colt narrowed his eyes, staring after him. "That's a first."

"Well, just let the man spend his time the way he

wants," Tammy said. "There's more to life than rodeo-ing." She cast a wink in Cissy's direction.

Colt scoffed, scowling good-naturedly at Cissy. "Whatever you done to my boy, you need to undo it soon. Otherwise, he's gonna be so out of shape he won't be able to throw his leg over the back of a bull."

This evoked a giggle despite her headache and queasy stomach. Cissy dropped her head and palmed the sides of the glass. It was still warm from Dominic's hand. She clutched it, savoring that bit of comfort.

"Is he good?" Cissy dragged her teeth over her bottom lip. "I mean, I know he's good. I've just never seen him ride before."

Jen released a wistful sigh. "Oh, girl, you've missed a real treat. No one rides a bull like Dominic."

"Hey, I resent that," Colt interjected, throwing a brawny arm across the back of Jen's chair. His lips twitched. "Though, I do gotta say, Dom's the best there is."

"The best ever." Tammy rose and piled up the dirty dishes before dropping them in the sink with a clank. "You really ought to check him out sometime." She raised her voice over the running water and squeezed a bottle of dishwashing liquid into the sink. "You and the boys could ride out with us on the next trip. I bet the twins would love it."

Cissy gripped the glass tighter, the warmth of Dominic's touch having faded. "Is it soon?" she asked, clarifying at Colt's bewildered glance, "The next trip?"

"A couple weeks or so," Colt said, running a hand through his blond hair. "In Atlanta. Not too bad of a drive."

Cissy lifted her eyebrows and smirked as Colt took a

swallow of Jen's coffee. She'd driven down that road before. And "not too bad" wasn't an accurate description.

"Some of the best bulls are supposed to be at this one," Colt added. "Chaos, Slammer. Those jokers can break your back."

Jen nudged Colt's broad chest with her elbow, muttering, "That's enough, Colt. You're scaring her."

Cissy followed Jen's eyes to the death grip she held on the glass. She relaxed her hold and settled back in the chair.

"Why does he do it?" Cissy wondered out loud. "Why do any of you do it when it's so dangerous?"

Colt grinned, a note of reverence coloring his tone. "Because it's a hell of a ride. Nothing else like it." He shrugged. "Some guys do it for fun. Some for money. Dom, well, he's just wild himself. Been that way since the day I met him. Lives like a hellion." He chuckled. "Like the damn sun's burning out and won't rise again."

He sobered, dropping back into his seat. Cissy squirmed under his scrutiny.

"Though, I gotta say, he's slowed down since I last saw him," he said. "Never known him to hang around home for so long."

Cissy's stomach dropped. Which meant it wouldn't be long before Dominic took off again. About two weeks, in fact. Her mind hung on that thought before snuffing it out and conjuring up Dominic's words from last night.

I want it all, Cissy. I want everything.

Whatever Dominic saw in her was attractive enough to draw him to her. Make him feel she had something valuable to offer him. Maybe that'd be reason enough for him to stay.

"Aunt Cissy!" The door banged a couple of times, shattering the comfortable silence at the table.

"Aunt Cissy," Kayden shouted, clutching a bundle at his middle and throwing himself into her arms. Jayden was hot on his heels, clambering up on Cissy's lap to hang on to her other side.

"There they are," Colt boomed, sexy smile and sunny disposition back on full blast. "Whatcha got there, man?"

Kayden pulled back and jerked his wrist out toward the floor. A long rope flicked out, knocking against the table leg and Jen's foot. She let loose a squeal.

"Sorry, Miss Jen." Kayden's jubilant expression was anything but. "Mr. Logan found me a new rope. And it's a long one, too."

"Is that right?" Cissy ran a hand through the soft layers of his hair, breathing him in. He smelled of fresh air and sunshine. And dirt.

"And Pop took us fishin' again down by the creek," Jayden added.

"We got to ride in a canoe." Kayden hastened to add, "We wore life persurvahs."

"Preservers," Cissy corrected.

Kayden shrugged. "Yeah, that."

"And we used crickets instead of worms." Jayden bounced on her left thigh, making her wince.

"And we roasted marshmallows." Kayden flicked the rope again.

"And Kayden got in trouble because he—"

"Hush, Jayden. Aunt Cissy don't want to hear all that." Kayden wrapped his arm around her neck and gave her a peck on the cheek. He whispered in her ear, "Mr. Logan said I wasn't bad. I asked him. He just said I was givin' him a run for his money." He pulled back, contemplating that. "You think he's gonna give me some allowance?"

Cissy cringed despite the humor in the situation. At least the others got a kick out of it. Laughter was on all sides of the table.

She tugged the boys in and hugged them close. Last night's fun aside, this was the highlight of her weekend. Having the boys here, healthy and happy. And she'd had a hand in that.

Her money pile had multiplied. She only needed two more weeks of wages to get her head fully above water. And she planned to use that money to start over and provide a safe, secure life for the boys.

How could she have forgotten that? Even for a second? She squeezed them tighter and kissed the tops of their heads.

"We missed you, Aunt Cissy." Kayden snuggled back up to her ear, his voice soft. "You'll go camping with us next time, won't you?"

"Of course."

"Good." Kayden examined her face for a moment, then tucked his small hands around her neck and leaned against her. "I knew you'd still be here. We're a team, right? Just like you said."

Cissy's heart clenched. She hadn't realized his uncertainty ran so deep. How had she not seen it?

Heat washed over her face and chest. Cissy firmed her mouth. She hadn't seen it because she'd been too concerned with her own uncertainties. Uncertainties that had seemed all consuming at the time but now held no weight.

Jason hadn't been completely wrong about her running from things. She had been running—from her fear of not being strong enough or good enough for the boys, fear of not being able to love them the way they deserved to be loved.

But she did love. And her love was valuable. The boys treasured it. And Dominic had asked for it almost as though he'd known…

Cissy straightened. It was time to follow through with something she'd been avoiding for several months now. Even before Crystal's death. She'd put it off long enough.

After breakfast, Cissy bustled the boys to her room and shooed them into the shower. They resisted, the long night of camping having left them tired and cranky. Eventually, they bargained for a bath instead. By that time, it no longer mattered. Just so long as it involved soap and water.

Jayden caught her wrist with a sudsy hand as she pushed up from the tub. "I told Kayden you'd still be here."

The trust on his smiling, upturned face strengthened her resolve.

Leaving the bathroom door open a crack, she made her way over to the nightstand and picked up her cell phone. Her heart skipped a beat as she plopped onto the edge of the bed. Her gaze strayed around the room, snagging on the closed bedroom door.

Her body came to life, humming with remembered pleasure. Dominic wanted it all. He wanted her love. And she was discovering she wanted to give it to him. But there was no way she could do that without taking care of the boys first.

Dominic wasn't the only one who wanted everything.

Kayden and Jayden did, too. They had to take priority over everyone—she couldn't imagine her life any other way. This was something she had to do. For her peace of mind. And, more important, for theirs. The boys needed to know they would be taken care of. And by whom.

Their delighted giggles drifted through the cracked door, punctuated by the splashes and squeaks of their bottoms scooting across the tub.

Cissy straightened and renewed her grip on the phone. No. She wouldn't allow Kayden and Jayden to continue to worry about where they belonged any longer than necessary.

Scrolling through her contacts, she found Jason's number and made the call.

DOMINIC EASED OFF DESTINY, speaking to the horse in soothing words as he untacked and settled her at the edge of the paddock. He paused for a moment and stroked the mare's neck. It'd been ages since he'd enjoyed a good, relaxing ride. And Destiny had delivered. She'd definitely earned a good rubdown.

"You done with that hose yet?" Dominic asked, glancing over his shoulder.

"In a minute."

Logan continued angling a spray of water over his horse's back. He followed each pass with his hand, smoothing out any matted clumps with gentle rubs. White foam slid over Logan's fingers with each pass.

The summer sun had beat down on them, causing the horses to sweat more than usual. The trail ride had gone smoothly. Only, Dominic had caught his mind drifting away from the chatter of the guests and lingering on thoughts of Cissy. How he'd rather be back at her side.

Back at the main house.

His gentle strokes along Destiny's back slowed. He couldn't remember the last time he'd actually wanted to be in Raintree's main house. Or at home for this long, come to think of it.

Colt was right. He had spent a lot of time off the circuit. And he was afraid the longer he stayed away, the harder it'd be to go back.

Brushing aside the nagging thoughts, Dominic studied Logan's movements. "You sure do baby him."

Logan didn't respond. Just kept up the methodical motions, rubbing out each sweat mark and making sure every strand of Lightning's hair was refreshed.

Logan pulled out more slack on the hose and lowered the pressure to a gentle stream. Lightning tilted his head to the side right before Logan reached up and glided a light sheen of water over his eyes, taking care to clean his face. Contrary to most horses, this one seemed to enjoy it.

"You take him out a lot?" Dominic asked.

"Almost every day. Mainly on the trails." Logan moved the spray to the horse's back again.

"He's gotten a lot calmer."

"He's always been calm."

"Not always. Used to be, Amy was the only one that could—" Dominic snapped his mouth shut. He'd gotten too comfortable. Forgotten some things were off-limits.

Logan's movements became jerky, sloshing the water in uneven patterns. His boots held a heavier tread on the ground when he stepped farther away and turned his back. Wasn't hard to read the signs. Every inch of his frame screamed, *Back off.*

Dominic sighed, stroking Destiny's back and weighing his options. It'd be easy to shrug this off. Give Logan his space and ignore the problem. He should just leave well enough alone.

Hell, he'd done exactly that for the past year. And before that, even. Kept a firm distance from his brother, his father and anything else that he couldn't ride out in eight seconds or less.

And damned if that didn't make it all the harder to bridge the gap.

Destiny's head jerked with a snort. Seemed more like a warning than encouragement. Still, he had trouble letting it slide. One of the main reasons for his return home had been Logan. He'd missed his brother like hell. Missed being able to talk to him. The more successful Dominic's rodeo career had become, the more his relationship with Logan had eroded. And at this point, there hadn't been much left to lose between them.

Dominic swept his chin over his shoulder, flinging off any regrets, and faced his brother. "You heard from her lately?"

Logan maintained his bullheaded silence. Back rigid, still rubbing that horse down.

Well, damn. He was all in now. Might as well meet the stubborn son of a gun head-on.

"You know," Dominic prodded. "Amy. Your wife."

"What the hell, Dom?" Logan swung around and glared. He kept his voice low, no doubt for the benefit of the horses, but fury blackened every word. "What'd I tell you when you swept back in here?"

"Not to stir shit up," Dominic recited.

"Right." Logan turned away.

"That's not how I see this, though."

Logan snapped back around. "Well, how do you see

it, then? Because the way I see it, you've been gone for more years put together than you've actually been here. So how the hell would you know anything about my life?"

"I know enough to see you're not happy. Can't be, not having Amy around. I also know it took two of y'all to get pregnant. You had a hand in that mistake as much as she did. And losing the baby wasn't her fault any more than it was yours."

Logan clenched his fists, chest rising on a sharp inhale. "I'm not discussing this with you."

"Why?"

"It's none of your business," he snapped.

"Should be. You're my brother. And Amy was more of a sister to me than any blood-born one could've been."

"I told you. This is none of—"

"How's it go, Logan? You ride Lightning every day? Treat him the way you should've treated her? Think if you love that horse of hers enough, she'll just appear one day?"

"All right." Logan flung the hose down, eyes flaring. "Long as we're getting in each other's business, let's talk about Cissy."

Dominic splayed his legs, digging his heels into the dirt. "Have at it."

"You taking to playing at home now instead of on the road?"

Dominic winced. That dagger hit its mark. "Watch that, Logan. I'm beginning to hate that damn word."

"What?" he mocked. "*Playing?* That's what you do isn't it? Play for a living? Play for fun? You haven't had a serious relationship with a woman in your entire life," Logan scoffed, chin jutting. He scuffed the ground with the toe of his boot. "Hell, you haven't had a serious relationship with anyone in your life. You just grace people with your presence long enough to get a smile, then haul ass to the next interstate. Forget about responsibilities or duty."

"And you're definitely the expert at those things, aren't you?" Dominic drawled. "Amy was a prime example. You only married her because she got pregnant. Followed through with your duty. Did pretty good until the occasion called for more than just fulfilling an obligation." The bite in his words gnawed his gut as well as his tongue. But damned if he could muzzle them. "You weren't the only one hurting. You had no right blaming her. And no right making her leave. So what if she didn't live up to your damned high standards? I sure as hell never have."

Logan's face darkened, his body drawing tight as a bow. Dominic tensed. For a moment, he expected his brother to land a fist in his gut. And he couldn't blame Logan. He deserved it.

He was beginning to think he should've just let it go. Not pushed or pried.

Logan hissed out a soft breath and dragged a hand over his face. The shadows hovering around his eyes deepened and spread, cloaking his entire body. He'd never looked so defeated. Or so alone. A stillborn baby and broken marriage had clearly taken its toll.

"I had good intentions toward Amy," Logan said, his voice husky. "No matter what you think you know, I did have the right intentions."

Dominic dropped his head. He wouldn't meet Logan's eyes. Couldn't face the pain in them. "I never said otherwise."

"I don't want you to say anything, dammit. I want you to listen." Logan's boots scraped over the ground on his approach. "I had good intentions. The best. Fact is, intentions don't always prosper. Sometimes the best intentions end up hurting the very ones you're trying to protect."

Dominic's head jerked up. "Is that what you think's going to happen with Cissy? Because that's not the road I'm taking with her."

"I'm just saying to tread carefully."

"I have no plans to hurt Cissy."

Logan laughed at that. Threw his head back and let the cynical chuckle taper off before peering at him again.

"The warning's not for her, baby brother. It's for you." His tone turned serious. "There's no guarantee on her end. She's not one of these girls you've known. The ones you've played around with. And I'm telling you, you better not proceed if you're not willing to follow through. Cissy's a strong woman. Knows her own mind. And she's not on her own, either."

Dominic waved a hand in the air. "You can rest your principles on that, Logan. I'm well aware those boys hang on her hip, and I've taken to them. I don't run screaming at the sight of kids."

"No. You don't. But you're also not in the habit of running toward them. I'm telling you, I don't see Cissy letting those boys take a backseat to anyone. And as long as I've known you, I've never seen you happy with anything but the driver's seat." Logan turned, gathering up Lightning's lead. "She might not intend to hurt you.

But if it came down to you or those boys, it'd take her a lot less than eight seconds to buck you off."

Dominic's limbs morphed into lead, pinning him in place as Logan passed on his way to the stables.

"I know you." Logan's expression softened as he took him in. "That kind of fall would break you in two, Dom."

Dominic struggled to find a rebuke, a defiant phrase or even a string of words that made a sentence. It proved impossible. His mouth ran dry, his tongue weak. Fears he didn't know he harbored gripped his throat. Insecurities clamored through his frame.

Bye, Dominic. That damned memory of his mother returned. The last time he saw her. On the day she'd discarded him for another man and a richer life.

Dominic clenched his eyes shut. Figured that memory would choose this moment to rear its ugly head again.

He spun back to Destiny and stroked her neck with a shaky hand. Leave it to Logan. Hardheaded fool was always looking at the negative side of things. Not to mention, he had a knack for tossing his two cents into everyone's corner.

Dominic shook his head. That was just Logan. Had a bad taste in his mouth and a broken heart. No blame could be laid there. It was what it was.

"He's just hurting, girl," he whispered, touching his forehead to Destiny's neck.

The horse snorted once more before nuzzling Dominic's arm.

"I know. About time for that cooldown, isn't it?"

Dominic retrieved the hose and began rinsing Destiny's legs, letting her get used to the spray. He shifted the hose from hand to hand and flexed his fingers. They still trembled.

A good man. That was what Cissy had said.

He rolled his shoulders, digging deeper into the task of cooling down the mare. Logan was right on one count. Cissy did know her own mind. And she'd settled it on who she thought he was.

But hell if he knew whether he could deliver. Or if he'd be enough.

Chapter Eight

"Come here."

Cissy gripped her knees, doubled over with laughter and tried to calm the excited breaths bursting from her lips. She tossed her hair out of her face, glancing up at an equally giddy Dominic.

"Come on over, baby," he called, crooking his fingers at her.

An adorable, boyish grin played with the curves of his mouth. His dark hair was mussed, his Stetson having fallen to the wayside long ago, and a wavy strand clung to his brow.

Blushes of pinks and reds from the setting sun glowed around him, painting him and the sprawling fields surrounding them with warmth that filled her chest. The day was just beginning to draw to a close. The top curve of the sun lingered on the edge of the horizon and floated a wave of gentle color around them as night reached out. Most of the guests had gone in for the evening meal, and the grounds were empty save for the small party still cackling behind her.

Cissy couldn't have imagined a more enjoyable day. The morning had been spent tending to the same routine chores but the temperature had rocketed past ninety-eight by two o'clock, prompting guests to cancel their trail rides and laze by the pool. As a result, Cissy spent the majority of the late Thursday afternoon turning the horses out. This was due, in most part, to Dominic's insistence. He'd pointed out it was time she and the boys got to know the other end of a horse for a change.

Kayden and Jayden had taken to the task with excitement and had enticed Tammy and Jen out, as well. Colt had turned up later and sparked a competition of hay bale jumping while the horses ran free in the field.

Cissy rose and eased into Dominic's arms, placing her hands to his chest. The strong breadth of it rose and fell on his soft chuckles. She rubbed her hands in circular motions, absorbing the solid, secure feel of him.

"You've got some hay here," Dominic murmured, reaching down to unwind a straw of it from her hair. The tips of his fingers lingered, smoothing over the strands. "You can tell you've been rolling around in it." His grin stretched into a devilish, dimpled smile. "Too bad it didn't get there the way I'd have preferred."

Cissy's heart skipped and her skin tingled. She bit her lip, casting a cautious glance over her shoulder at the group behind them.

Colt balanced on top of a large stack of hay bales several feet off, taunting the crew scaling their way over to him. Kayden and Jayden clung to Tammy and Jen. The pairs sprung from one stack to the next, shoes slipping on the slick sides and fingers digging into the thick stacks to hold on. Squeals of delight abounded with each successful jump, their attention concentrated on the task at hand.

Satisfied they were otherwise occupied, Cissy turned back to Dominic and rose to her toes, brushing her mouth over the stubble lining his jaw. The rough texture of his five-o'clock shadow and earthy, male scent had her rubbing her cheek against his with a soft sigh.

She nuzzled her nose into Dominic's tanned throat and smiled against his skin. It had become clear to everyone early on that she wasn't talented at scaling hay bales. She'd fallen more times than she could count, Dominic's careful grip preventing her from slamming into the ground on several occasions.

Dominic pulled her closer, folding her in and caressing her back. His throaty murmur vibrated against her smile. "We could always come back out later. Settle on top of one of those bales and count the stars."

Cissy drew back, contentment streaming through her blood. "Really?"

"Yeah." His warm palms drifted down to settle on the upper curve of her bottom. "Just us. It'll be cooler by then."

Another surge of delight swept through her. Some things would be cooler. But if the pleasurable waves sweeping through her body were any indication, some things wouldn't.

She felt Dominic's pull inside her. Right where he'd said he wanted to be. His fingers wrapped firmer around her heartstrings with each passing hour and tugged without pause. He kept pulling her closer and closer until her days began and ended on thoughts of him.

The experience was both scary and exciting.

"I got the farthest this time, Mr. Dominic." Jayden bounded toward them, his words bursting out in small gasps.

Dominic eased his hold on her and stepped away to

scoop Jayden up in his arms and prop him on his hip. "Good deal, Jayden."

"That's only because I was helping Miss Jen," Kayden said. Not to be outdone, he wrapped himself around Dominic's leg and looked up at him with a grave expression. "If I'd been on my own, I could've gone faster. Girls mess up everything."

Dominic laughed and ruffled his blond hair. "You both went fast enough. Besides, it's not so bad having a girl around. Matter of fact, I think you would've bit the dirt a time or two if Miss Jen hadn't been looking out for you."

Kayden mulled that over for a second. "I guess," he conceded. "Did you know Miss Jen races horses at the rodeo?"

"Yep," Dominic said. "She's good."

"Does she ride the bulls, too?" Jayden asked.

"Course not," Kayden declared. "Girls can't ride bulls."

"Well, now, some can," Dominic said, setting Jayden down and smiling when he latched on to his free leg. "I've seen one ride before."

"Bet she didn't stay on long," Kayden said.

"Nah. But none of us, boy or girl, stay on very long to begin with," Dominic added.

"I bet Aunt Cissy could do it." Jayden released Dominic's leg and darted over to wrap around hers.

Dominic winked. "I tend to agree with you, buddy. I don't think your Aunt Cissy would have any trouble handling a bull. Matter of fact, she could do just about anything she turned her mind to."

"I don't know about that," Cissy returned. She busied

herself with picking hay out of Jayden's hair and dropping a kiss on his head. "But I'm flattered you think so."

"When are you gonna ride a bull again, Mr. Dominic?" Kayden asked.

Cissy froze. Leave it to Kayden to get right to it. She and Dominic hadn't discussed the future in any capacity since that night in her room a couple of weeks ago. She was wary of broaching the subject and suspected Dominic was, too.

She licked her bottom lip and examined Dominic's expression. He met her eyes briefly before dodging her gaze and detaching Kayden from his leg.

"Soon," he said. He spun Kayden back toward the hay bales and gently tapped his bottom. "Why don't you two give the bale jumping another shot? This time without Miss Jen, and see how many you can get across."

"Okay." Kayden beckoned over his shoulder. "Come on, Jayden. You count the bales for me and then I'll do it for you."

The two took off toward the string of hay bales with a new challenge. The others had wandered off to plop on the ground and rest.

Cissy brushed a bit of grass from her knee. "Colt mentioned there was an event coming up soon." She picked at the dirt under her fingernails and waited. *Stay cool. Don't make a big deal out of it.* Maybe if she eased into it, he wouldn't feel obligated. "I wasn't sure if—"

"Aunt Cissy, ask Pop to come count for us, okay, please?" Kayden's gleeful yell interrupted, forcing Cissy to pull her attention from Dominic.

Pop's tall figure ambled toward them across the field. He drew closer, his normally relaxed expression holding a note of tension. He halted when he reached them, surveying the boys laughing and jumping bales behind them before facing Cissy with drawn brows. "You expecting someone?"

Cissy tensed. The hum of relaxed enjoyment dwindled. She was expecting someone. But not until tomorrow. It was just like Jason to show up on his own terms.

Shoving her hands into her pockets, she conjured up a tight smile and nodded. "Jason."

Pop eyed the boys squealing behind her. "The boys' father?"

"Yeah. I called a few days ago and asked if he could come meet me. I need to settle some things."

Dominic surveyed her for a moment. "You sure that was a good idea?"

"It has to be done at some point. Might as well be now."

"Well," Pop interjected, "he's waiting in the office with Logan. You best go on up. I'll take the boys and get 'em fed. You take your time." He brushed past them to join the group now clustered around the hay bales.

"Boys," Cissy called. "I have to go take care of something. Pop's gonna take you in. Be good for him, all right?"

"Okay, Aunt Cissy," Jayden hollered back with a wave.

Kayden spared her a quick glance, bouncing on a bale and whooping out, "Sure."

Cissy moved swiftly across the field. The sun had dipped well below the horizon now, the rosy glow having faded and disappeared. The gradual darkness made it difficult to see the smudged outline of the path she followed back to the main house.

She focused on the porch lights blazing up ahead and

tried to fight off the quivers rippling through her belly. The sound of Dominic's heavy steps falling close behind her brought a sense of comfort while at the same time heightening her anxiety.

Half-afraid he'd continue and half-afraid he'd stop, she said, "You don't have to come with me, you know."

"I know."

The calm tenor of his voice and the finality of his words soothed her nerves. Her chin lifted with renewed determination. She'd see this through to the bitter end. And, thank God, it seemed she was about there.

They arrived sooner than she'd anticipated, the shiny metal of the doorknob twisting smoothly under her hand. She swept the door open and entered the room.

The stale odor of cigarette smoke filled her nostrils. Jason lounged in a chair opposite Logan at the mahogany desk, his long limbs stretched out. His blond hair was mussed and sticking up at odd angles, as though he'd run his hands through it several times.

Jason's head swiveled, gaze landing on Cissy. His face lifted for a moment, pleasure lighting his eyes and curling his lips. But a moment later, it fell with disappointment.

"Damn. I always forget." Jason hunched forward, then rose with a frown. He took a deep drag from the cigarette poised between his fingers. Smoke escaped on his rough exhalation and he muttered with a pained sigh, "You look exactly like her."

Cissy tightened her mouth, ignoring the wobble in her chin. The reminder of what she'd lost hit harder than it ever had before. And it wouldn't do to fall apart now. No matter how much she missed Crystal.

"It's good to see you too, Jason," Cissy whispered, digging deep to find a thread of anger rather than grief.

Jason examined her, his frown deepening. His mouth opened soundlessly before he winced. Without pause, he crossed the room.

Cissy blinked with surprise when his hand cupped the back of her head. He placed a gentle kiss to her forehead and rolled his own against hers. His hand kneaded the back of her neck and he whispered, "Sorry. I just miss her."

Her vision blurred, eyes flooding. Was this how he'd handled Crystal? With such tenderness? It must be his worry or his grief that brought it on. Cissy had never been privy to this side of him before.

Disconcerted by the drop of her guard, Cissy drew back and disentangled from his touch. It was easier to remember the way he was on a regular basis. Moody. Closed and unapproachable.

"They don't smoke in here, Jason," she said, eyeing the cigarette still dangling between his fingers at his side.

He stiffened and shook his head. After taking one more drag, he stubbed it out on the heel of his shoe and dropped it in the trash can. He propped himself on the edge of the desk and crossed one ankle over the other.

"So," Jason said, spreading his arms, "I'm here. Where are the boys?"

"They're being taken care of. I didn't ask you here to get them. I asked you here to talk. I wanted—" Her voice failed her, cracking on the next syllable. She cleared her throat and stated with determination, "I want to talk to you about the adoption."

Jason shifted. His hands curled over the edge of the

desk as he exchanged looks with Dominic and Logan. "Can we have some privacy?"

"This is as private as it's gonna get," Dominic said, stepping closer and placing a hand on her shoulder.

Jason's knuckles turned white. He smiled and asked, "Got yourself some reinforcements, Cissy?"

She slipped from under Dominic's touch, casting him an apologetic glance.

"There's no need for reinforcements," she said. "I'm not trying to force you into anything. I just want you to listen to me. Really listen and try to understand what I'm asking of you."

Jason's smile dissolved. He lowered his chin and nodded.

Cissy rubbed her fingertips on the hem of her shorts, then squared her shoulders.

"I've thought about what you said and my position hasn't changed. You can probably guess what I'm going to ask." She hesitated at his frozen silence before forging ahead. "I don't want you to sign the boys over for adoption. Instead, I want you to sign them over to me. Permanently."

The air in the room grew heavy, the smoke lingering and casting a haze around them. Jason's eyes narrowed and a sneer marked his face. His low words vibrated. "You still trying to take my boys?"

Cissy shook her head. "I'm not taking anything that doesn't belong to me. They're my nephews, and I have some say in what happens to them."

"I'm their father. I have the final say in what happens to them—"

"Their father?" Cissy's body jerked, her feet stalking forward. "You haven't been a father to them. You've been a sporadic tourist. Popping in and out of their lives whenever it suited you."

Jason shoved off the desk, glowering down at her. "Don't start with that shit again, Cissy. We've been down that road before. I've explained that I wasn't ready for kids—"

She held up a hand. "I know, I know. You've spun the tale before. For God's sake, I could recite it from memory." Fury returned, boiling in her blood and spewing from her mouth. "I'm sick to death of it. And so was Crystal. So much so, that she finally came to her senses in the end and begged me to intervene. You have no idea how hard that was for her. She lay on that bed knowing she was dying and had no choice but to admit to herself that you would never pull through for your sons. You can't possibly imagine how much she suffered over that."

"Stop it," he demanded.

"I wish I could. But you weren't there, Jason." Her vision blurred. She blinked furiously, forcing back the tears. "You weren't even there at the end. When she needed you the mos—"

"Stop," Jason choked, pressing a fist to his mouth and staggering to the window. He dragged his hands through his hair and gripped the back of his neck. "You're so damned judgmental. So unforgiving." He jerked back to face her, his voice hoarse. "Did it ever occur to you that it was too hard for me? That it was too much to just sit there and watch her..." He swallowed hard. "Not everyone's as strong as you, Cissy. I loved her more than I've loved anyone in my life but I couldn't do that. I couldn't watch her day in and day out getting weaker and weaker. Or stay in that hospital.

The smell of death everywhere—" His voice broke. "I tried. God knows I tried. But she knew. And she asked me not to come anymore." His eyes blazed. "And damn you for interfering in what we had. What was private. You had no place in it."

Heat suffused Cissy's face. She'd let her prejudice and ill will for him override her compassion. Not once had she given a thought to how difficult Crystal's illness must have been for him. All else aside, Jason had always been honest about his love for Crystal.

She bit her lip and dropped her head, wishing she could crawl right under the wood planks of the floor and disappear into the dark.

Clearing her throat, she said, "I'm sorry." She forced herself to meet his eyes and gestured helplessly. "I didn't know. She never told me. And I'm sure it was as difficult for you as it was for me. I know you loved her," she added softly. "She never doubted that."

Jason's shoulders dropped. He dragged his palms over his face, then muttered, "So spell it out. What exactly are you planning?"

"I'm going to give them security and a good home. And I'll make sure they grow up happy and provided for," she said in a soft voice. "They'll know they're wanted."

He squeezed his eyes shut and clenched his jaw.

Cissy continued gently, "You were ready to give them over to someone you didn't know. Why not give them to me?"

"Why not?" He opened his eyes and smiled sadly. "Because we're cut from the same cloth. We were born scrapping for every damn thing. Things don't just happen for people like us." His lip curled. "And you think you can just step in and make everything good? That my boys would be better off with you? You know enough about how the world works. You and I both know the score."

Cissy flinched. Jason was so blunt. He never shied away from calling things the way he saw them. She couldn't fault him for his honesty.

He was right. Nothing had ever come to her easily. She'd had to scrape and scrounge for what little she had. It was a good rule of thumb to keep expectations low. She'd learned to never hope for better. To never trust others. And never take risks.

She'd lived alone. That way no one could disappoint her. And she couldn't disappoint them.

Jason shoved his hands into his pockets, dragging out a cigarette pack and lighter. His hands trembled and he turned each item over and over in his palms as if seeking something to hold on to.

He looked up at her then. His eyes weak and empty.

Her heart bled for him, her body sagging. That was the choice she faced. An independent life void of complications or obligations. A life of meaningless days and nights with no one to share them and no one to love.

Or a life full of responsibilities and challenges, but at the same time, delightful surprises. Laughter. And more love than she'd ever known.

"You're right," Cissy conceded. "I lived like that for a long time. Accepting just what I was given, not expecting anything better. But I no longer want to live like that. I want the boys to have the best. I love them. And I'll make sure they feel loved. I can take care of them and do right by them. If you'll give me the chance."

"How will you do that, Cissy? You've got no money,

no home." Jason jerked his chin toward Dominic. "Unless you plan on taking charity here indefinitely."

"When have you ever known me to do that? I've worked hard over the past couple of months. I know what needs to be done and I'm doing it. I've even been thinking about going back to school so I can earn better money. Have other options."

Jason scoffed. "That'd be hard enough on your own. Forget doing it with two kids."

"Lots of people do it every day. Why not me? Being a parent isn't the end of the world."

Cissy's muscles relaxed. She paused, surprised by the sweep of pride that moved through her. Before, she'd had to reason that argument out. Had to talk herself into believing it. Now it was a comforting truth.

"As a matter of fact," she continued, "it's a beginning." Her neck warmed—in the exact spots where Kayden and Jayden always placed their small hands when hugging her. "The best kind of beginning."

Jason examined her, his expression inscrutable.

"Please," Cissy pleaded. "I swear I won't let them down. Please give me the chance I wasn't willing to give you."

His hands tightened, fisting at his sides. Light glinted over the moisture in his eyes. He jerked his head with a nod, then took rough steps toward the door.

Cissy breathed a soft sigh of relief. She wrapped her fingers around Jason's arm as he passed, stilling him and seeking out his eyes. "Thank you, Jason."

He pulled away, opening the door and disappearing around the corner.

Cissy took a step forward, wanting to follow and

offer him something more. Comfort…gratitude… *something.*

Dominic blocked her path, his big body brushing hers. "I'll see him out." He hovered on the threshold, dark eyes lingering on her, then turned and left.

Cissy's stomach dropped, her relief dissipating. Dominic had never looked at her that way before. There was something behind his eyes. Something she couldn't place but felt all the same.

She turned to find Logan staring at the empty doorway. His gaze shifted then, and he caught her trying to read his expression. He dropped his head and shuffled a few papers around on the desk.

At her refusal to look away, he sighed, leaning into his palms and facing her head-on. "It's late, Cissy. The boys will be looking for you."

"It had to be done."

"Yeah. It did." He smiled. Gentle and sad. "And it took a lot of guts. It's a difficult situation on all sides. Those boys are lucky to have you."

She nodded. There was no question she'd done the right thing for the boys. Her steps slowed at the door, her mind turning over the look Dominic had given her, testing it from different angles. Her throat tightened on the question rising from her chest but it managed to escape.

"Will he stay?"

"You made things plain," Logan said. "Everything's settled. There's no reason for him to unless he wants to see the boys one last time."

"No." She should stop now. While she was ahead. "I meant Dominic. Do you think he'll stay?"

Logan hesitated. "I don't know." His tone turned apologetic. "But I've learned not to expect it."

Cissy stilled. "That's a good rule of thumb," she whispered.

"What?"

"Nothing," she muttered.

Cissy shook her head and crossed the threshold to make her way to her room. She'd think about that later. Right now, she needed to talk to the boys and begin preparations for their future. She just hoped Dominic wanted to be a part of it.

"MIND IF I have a smoke before I leave?"

Dominic eased the screen door shut behind him with his heel. Jason leaned on the white porch rail, staring at the ground below. He didn't look up to see Dominic's nod but proceeded to dig a cigarette out of the pack in his hand all the same. His hands trembled as he lit it, snapping the lighter's wheel several times before it sparked and issued a flame.

Jason took a deep pull before finally glancing at him from the corner of his eye. He exhaled a curl of smoke and held the cigarettes out. Dominic shook his head. Jason dropped the pack to his side. The hum of crickets and cicadas hung on the night air wrapping around them.

"This your ranch?"

Still silent, Dominic nodded. He couldn't, for the life of him, find any words that fit the occasion.

"You're that bull rider, yeah?" Jason shoved the lighter and cigarette pack into his pocket. "The one that got World past four years. Up for it again this year. Dom Slade, right?"

"Yeah." Dominic maintained his stance a few feet away.

Jason laughed. It was weak and short-lived. "That's

some crazy shit y'all do, man. Never met anyone before that actually did it." He straightened from the rail and turned. "Course, not a lot of people really get what I do, either. Cissy tell you?"

"No."

He took another pull on his cigarette. "Didn't think so. Probably never talks about me." Ashes flicked as his fingers thumped with nervous motions. "I'm a drummer and a singer. Spend most of my time traveling for gigs and what's left looking for them. Wake up in one state and go to sleep in another. Don't know which end is up some days."

"That I can understand," Dominic said.

"Uh-huh. You probably do your share of traveling, too." Jason hesitated, chewing on his lower lip. "My boys doing good?"

Dominic peered into the darkness beyond the house. "They're doing great."

Jason bobbed his head several times before scrubbing the toe of his shoe over the porch floor. "I shouldn't say that." He looked up. "*My boys*. They're not mine anymore."

Dominic reluctantly faced him. "Cissy will take good care of them. They're happy with her."

Jason leaned back on the porch rail with his elbows, splaying his hands out almost as if to steady them and studying the red glow of his cigarette. "Think I'm a loser, Dom?"

Dominic's chest swelled with sympathy. At the same time, his shoulders stiffened. It was obvious Jason cared about his sons. But he was still willing to walk away from his own flesh and blood. That he couldn't understand. He couldn't wrap his head around that bit.

"Think I'm worthless because I don't want my kids?" Jason's eyes narrowed, his expression guarded.

"No one's saying that."

"Cissy's saying it," Jason shot back. "Doing more than saying it. She's acting on it."

"She loves those boys. She's just doing what she thinks is best for them."

"So she says," Jason grunted. "I tell you, it'd be a hell of a lot easier to hand them over to someone else. A stranger. Someone I didn't know. Hell, anyone else. Just as long as it wasn't Cissy." His lip curled. "That's a damned blow to a man's pride, you know? A woman doing what you can't. Making something out of nothing. Not even needing you."

Dominic froze.

Bye, Dominic.

Dominic spun, gripping the screen door's handle. "I don't think I'm the best one to talk to about this—"

"Why?" Jason stepped forward, flicking the tip of his cigarette again. A spray of red ash hit the porch. "Thought you'd be the one to understand. Career minded. A fellow nomad. Don't think I'm proud of leaving them. I'm not. Wish I felt differently about it. But the bitch of it all is, I never chose this life. It just chose me. You can't change who you are. You're not meant to."

A queasiness settled in Dominic's gut. How many times had he consoled himself with that same argument when he'd left the ranch for another rodeo? When he'd wished he was more like Logan? Solid and stable?

The black handle of the screen door slipped from his grip.

"And what's wrong with that?" Jason continued. "When you're honest about it? I told Crystal that in the very beginning. Told her putting down roots wasn't for everyone. Wasn't even the life for her. But she tried anyway. Every time I came back to her, I told her—must've been a thousand times—that she was going against the grain. Turning on her God-given nature. She wasn't cut out to be a mom any more than I was to be a dad. I think the boys even knew it."

He scoffed, pausing to take another deep drag. "That's why Cissy and I always fought like hell. Always knew Cissy was worth more to those boys than me. Hell, Crystal and I put it together, even." His face scrunched with disgust. "I couldn't stomach the thought of her having my boys. Showin' me up. But I never really had a chance to begin with. I loved Crystal. God knows I did. And I loved those boys, too. It's just, some men aren't built for it. At least I'm man enough to admit that."

Every muscle in Dominic's body seized.

A good man.

Cissy's words returned. Though, this time, they came without the usual rush of pride and pleasure. They seemed foreign. Incomprehensible and unattainable.

Jason's cynical laugh drew his attention once more. "Maybe you don't want to talk because you got your own dealings with Cissy."

Jason waited for a response. When he didn't receive one, he took one last pull on the cigarette, stubbed it out on the porch rail and threw the butt into the grass. He worked his way down the steps, pausing at the bottom and turning back.

"I'm not a bad guy, Dom. I just have other ambitions." He smiled then. Wide and genuine. "Good luck with Cissy and those high standards of hers. Because you're damn sure gonna need it."

Dominic watched him stroll to his car, slide in and pull off. He kept watching until the red taillights faded into dots then disappeared into the night.

It was late. Cissy would be inside waiting for him. The boys, too. Waiting for a last bit of fun with him before being sent to bed. He should make his way back in.

Dominic rolled his shoulders, trying to shake off that nagging feeling. It didn't help, though.

A good man. That was how Cissy saw him. Yet she saw the complete opposite in Jason. A guy Dominic initially thought must be akin to a demon from hell to be able to walk away from his kids. As it was, Jason had turned out to be just an ordinary guy. One who didn't think he was cut out for being a parent. And one who felt that loss keenly.

A good man. That was what Cissy had said.

Dominic tilted his head back and inhaled. The summer night mocked him. The cicadas rattled, the hiss and snap booming in his ears and driving deep into his bones. He turned and opened the door. But he couldn't quite make his way through it.

Jason had made more points than he'd like to admit. And after their conversation, the lines dividing him from Jason had been blurred if not erased.

If that were the case, what did Cissy see in him that made him any different from Jason?

And was there really any difference to begin with?

Chapter Nine

CLICK HERE TO APPLY.

Cissy followed the link on the web page and clicked the mouse. A new window sprang open, revealing a two-page application for an online program with a Georgia college about three hours away from Raintree Ranch. The printer whirred on the table to her left, nudging out a paper copy.

"You did another one, Aunt Cissy?" Kayden slapped a book against his thigh and peered at the pages spitting out of the printer.

"Just one more, then we need to go." She smiled and rose to squeeze his shoulder before retrieving the papers.

Kayden groaned, flouncing across the library to flop into one of the children's chairs. "More? Crud. We've been here for forever."

"Come on, Kayden," Tammy admonished, patting his head and settling on the colorful rug in front of him. "It's your aunt Cissy's day off. Let her do something she'd like to do for a change."

Jayden rounded a book aisle, clutching an armful of books and sat down beside Kayden. "I don't want to go yet," he said, flipping through pages. "There's some more books I want to look at."

"You've looked at all of them already," Kayden complained. "If you get any more, we won't fit in the car."

Cissy conjured up a stern expression and stifled a grin. "That's enough, Kayden. He can look at as many books as he wants. Just remember, Jayden, you can only take two with you today."

"Yes, ma'am," he said. "But can't we stay longer? Just so I can look?"

Cissy sighed. She hated to cut their first library visit short but she was anxious to get back to Raintree. They'd spent the majority of the morning running errands. The most important of which was picking up their newly repaired Toyota.

Her hand drifted to her pocket, patting it and smiling at the clink of keys. She'd asked Tammy to give them a lift to town so she could settle the bill with Logan's mechanic friend. Cissy had barely been able to contain her excitement when she'd placed the short stack of bills in the man's hand. After he'd passed her the keys, she'd shaken his hand so hard Tammy had intervened for fear she'd break it.

The poor old Toyota had bounced and swayed when she and the boys had piled in, smiles on all of their faces. The beat-up car wasn't much, but it was theirs. The boys now had a safe mode of transportation and she'd been the one to provide it for them. She couldn't remember ever feeling so accomplished. It seemed a small step but had turned out to mean so much more.

A drift of cool air blowing from a vent at her feet lifted the edge of the papers in her hand. The empty boxes on the college application beckoned up at her to fill them in. Her fingers hovered over the pages, itching to grab a pen and begin.

She couldn't quite yet, though. There was something greater that needed to be decided before she could take the next step. She had several college applications. Some of them on campus and some online. Which one she'd decide to enroll in would all depend on Dominic. That, and whether she and the boys would remain at Raintree or move on to settle somewhere else.

Her knees almost buckled beneath her. Leaving Raintree Ranch was not a pleasant thought. Or one she'd seriously scrutinized. But if things didn't go the way she hoped they would with Dominic, it might be her only option.

"Aunt Cissy, please?" Jayden's heels bounced against the floor when she told him it was time to go.

"We really need to get back to the ranch, baby."

Good grief, did they ever. The weekend of the rodeo in Atlanta had run up on her before she'd had a chance to realize it. She'd been preoccupied with the legal proceedings related to terminating Jason's parental rights. Each day had been filled to the brim with the grind of ranch chores, paperwork and meetings. So much so, that she hadn't had a chance to steal a moment with Dominic.

No. That wasn't altogether accurate. In actuality, she'd been delaying the conversation about their future together for as long as possible in hopes that Dominic would choose to bring it up. Or, even better, that he would inform her he was sitting this rodeo out—then there'd be no need to discuss it at all…yet.

That, however, wasn't to be. Colt and Jen had chattered about the competition nonstop last night at dinner, barely pausing to take a bite of food. Cissy had hoped Dominic would voice a protest or declare he wasn't going, but he'd remained silent and, to her dismay, only met her eyes once during the hour-long family meal.

What unnerved her even more was the fact that Dominic had been uncharacteristically reserved since Jason's visit. Which made it all the more vital for her to touch base with him as soon as possible.

"I don't mind staying awhile longer with the boys, Cissy," Tammy said, breaking through her thoughts. She pushed one of the books closer to Jayden's busy hands. "That way Jayden can look at a few more and then I could take them out for ice cream on the way back, maybe?"

Kayden sprang upright at that. "Can we, Aunt Cissy? Can we?"

Tammy laughed and thumped the toe of his shoe. "You gotta behave though, young man. I can't have you stressing me out right before an event."

Kayden nodded eagerly. "Yes, ma'am." He whirled back around. "Come on, Aunt Cissy, can we?"

"Well, I suppose. If it's not too much trouble, Tammy?"

"Of course not," she said, grinning. "I can get one last twin fix before I leave."

"What time are you leaving?" Cissy asked.

"I'm packing tomorrow morning and leaving around noon. Jen and I had originally planned on leaving with Colt and Dom but they're taking off tonight." She made a face. "You know men. They like to scope out the lay of the land, so to speak, before the competition."

Cissy frowned, clutching the papers tighter. Well, that answered one of her questions. Dominic was defi-

nitely going. So this was it. Either she took a chance.
A chance on love. And on Dominic. Or she went with
the only other alternative. Which was to remain silent
and let him leave. Without ever knowing if they had a
real shot.

"It would really help me out if you're sure you don't
mind," Cissy said. At Tammy's nod, she gathered up
the packets of information she'd printed. "Boys, I'll see
you tonight at dinner. Be on your best behavior for Ms.
Tammy, okay?"

They "yes, ma'am-ed" her in unison. She dropped a
kiss on each of their foreheads before tossing Tammy a
grateful smile and heading out to the Toyota. The drive
back to the ranch was riddled with doubts and unset-
tling questions.

Dominic had asked her for this, but how would he
respond when he finally heard it? Would he welcome
it? Or was she assuming this was what he wanted from
her? Maybe this wasn't what he'd asked for at all. Maybe
she was expecting too much. And what if this scared
him off?

Cissy tossed her hair back from her face and pressed
her foot down harder on the pedal. There was no way
she'd misunderstood. Dominic couldn't have been
clearer. He wanted something real with her. Something
permanent.

Her stomach roiled. Dominic may have asked for
something permanent with her. But he'd never mentioned the boys. Did what he was asking for involve
something permanent with them?

She stifled a curse. This was ridiculous. She was
being ridiculous, looking for problems where there were
none. She'd seen Dominic with Kayden and Jayden. He

cared for them. Enjoyed being with them. And, more often than not, he came up with excuses to spend time with them.

Dominic was nothing like all the other men she'd known. That was one of the first things she'd learned about him. He wouldn't have asked for so much from her if he wasn't willing to give her as much in return.

Even though she chose to focus on the more positive thoughts, her mood swung between excited anticipation and debilitating fear. Cissy found the latter won out as she stood at the door to Dominic's bunkhouse twenty minutes later.

Shifting from one foot to the other, she glanced around, half expecting someone to spring from the side of the building and call her a coward. She hesitated, turning away for a moment and toying with the idea of returning to the main house.

Just go, Cissy, a tiny voice urged. *He'll never know you were even here.*

She spun back around and firmed her stance. That was the exact reason she shouldn't back out. Dominic would never know she was here, but she would. She'd know it every time she regretted walking away or not speaking up.

Just as Jason had known it when he'd decided to leave the boys. She'd seen it in his eyes when he'd sparred with her in the office. It had filled his expression and saturated every line of him. He'd ended up emptier than he'd ever been after that moment.

Cissy lifted her chin. Jason may have not learned from his mistakes but she had. She wasn't going to let another opportunity for happiness just slip on by.

Raising a fist, she rapped her knuckles on the door.

"It's open." Dominic's muffled voice just managed to reach outside.

She twisted the knob with a shaky hand and entered. Immediately, Dominic's woodsy scent enveloped her, warming her skin. She remained still for a moment, glancing around. The kitchen and living area were small but adequate and tidy. A coffee mug sat on the table by a recliner. A TV sounded low on the other side of the room, issuing forth a recitation of PBR statistics and standings.

"You packed yet?" Dominic's deep rumble drifted in from an adjoining room.

Cissy swallowed the lump in her throat and rounded the corner. The fresh scent of soap and shampoo lingered in the moist air at the threshold. A black overnight bag yawned open on a rumpled bed. Clanks and clunks of items being shuffled around sounded from the bathroom.

"I'm planning on leaving on time, Colt."

The bathroom door swung open and Dominic emerged, his muscular bulk filling the doorway and his tanned hand rasping the zipper shut on a shaving bag. A pair of faded jeans hung, unbuttoned, low on his slim hips. His feet and chest were bare and his damp hair stuck up in adorable, dark tufts on his head as though he'd just rubbed a towel over it.

"I mean it. I'm not waiting on your slow…"

Dominic's words trailed off when he looked up. His expression lit with surprise, then relaxed into a pleased smile. "Cissy." His eyes darkened with confusion as he examined her expression. "Is something wrong? The boys okay?"

"Yeah." She licked her lips, dragging her eyes from

the black sprinkling of hair that arrowed down his sculpted abs and returned her gaze to his face. "Fine." She swallowed again. "With Tammy."

Get it together. At least make a full sentence.

"I mean, the boys are fine." She forged ahead before her tongue tied again. "I needed to ask you something."

"Okay." He tossed the shaving bag on the bed then turned to start back to the bathroom. "Just let me grab a shirt—"

"No. Wait. I need to do this now." Cringing, she wrung her hands together. "Please? Can I just get this out first?"

He spun back around and waited, arms hanging at his sides.

"We went and picked up my car this morning. It's in good shape now." She shrugged. "Well, at least, as in good a shape as it's going to get. And I paid the work off, so, there's that. Which led me to think about the next step." She squared her shoulders. "I've given it some thought and I want to do something with my life. You know, something more?"

Dominic moved slowly, his hands slipping into his pockets and his chiseled jaw tightening.

"I've looked at a lot of degree programs and there's a couple different ways I can go about it. I could get an apartment near a college campus and take a few night classes. Or I could do an online program and basically do course work whenever I wanted. Wherever I wanted. Which is what I want to ask you about." Her heart thundered and her mouth went dry. "I wanted to ask you…"

Dear Lord, there had to be a way to ask. An easy, face-saving way to ask if he wanted her to stay or go. And then it occurred to her, her heart slowing. It didn't matter what his answer was. It wouldn't change how she felt. No matter whether she stayed or went. She'd still feel the same.

There was no need to ask. Only to tell.

"No, that's wrong," she whispered. "I don't need to ask you anything. I need to tell you something."

He relaxed slightly, muscular abs and chest rippling on release. "Okay."

"And before I say it, I want to point out that it's day-time." She gestured toward the light slipping through the blinds in the window. "And that I haven't been drinking. And know exactly what I'm doing."

Dominic smiled and shook his head. "Cissy, what is it you want to say?"

"You have it." The words burst from her lips. Her nerves clamored, shaking her frame.

"Have what?" He crossed to her side, concern flooding his features. Taking her upper arms in his hands, he murmured, "Relax. What exactly is it I have?"

She reached up and moved his hands. "You have it," she whispered, placing one of his palms over her heart and the other at her temple. "You're here, you see?"

Understanding dawned in his eyes. It gave her the courage to finish.

"I love you. That's what I needed to tell you. That's all," she mumbled.

His gaze roved over her face, lingering on her mouth. "That's all?"

The words held a note of wonder and were so soft she barely caught them. She moved to answer but Dominic cut her reply short. He dropped his head and parted her lips with his own, sweeping his tongue deep into the recesses of her mouth.

Her body hummed, longing streaming through her veins and urging her closer. She stepped forward and pressed her chest to his. The hard heat of him seeped into her breasts and spread over her skin.

His fingers stroked into her hair, gripping the back of her head, sending tingles over her scalp and down her neck. He pulled back, dark eyes clinging to hers as he shook his head from side to side and whispered, "That's all?"

Waves of sensation pounded in her blood. She wrapped her hand around his neck and brought his mouth to hers again, pouring all her love into it. Into him. His soft sigh of pleasure enveloped her before his strong arms did the same, drawing her in so there wasn't an inch of space between them.

Cissy vaguely registered Dominic's movements as he reached around her to sweep the bags from the bed. He toppled them onto it, removing her clothes and pausing to brush his mouth over every inch of her skin as he went.

She tugged at his jeans and he lifted his hips, assisting her in pushing them down his legs and off the bed with her toes, then rolled to his back to clasp her on top of him. Her eyes drifted closed as his calloused palms swept back up her legs, cupping her calves and the backs of her thighs. They smoothed over the curves of her bottom and drifted over the line of her spine.

Trembling, she ran her hands over his body, the sprinkling of dark hair on his chest and abdomen rasping against her fingers. She bit her lip on a rush of excitement as she moved her hand over the hard length of him, then absorbed his soft moan with her mouth.

His hands stilled, curling over her shoulders and lifting her away from him.

"Please," she whispered. She teased his lips with nips of her teeth before kissing the strong column of his throat. "Please..."

"Tell me what you like." His hoarse voice was strained. He swept her hair back with a trembling hand, cupping her cheek and tilting her face to his. His face flushed with passion as he searched her eyes. "Just tell me and I'll give it to you. What do you want?"

Vulnerability resided in every tautened muscle of his body. The sensuous curve of his mouth firmed in determination but his long limbs shook against her. There was no mistaking the yearning in his gaze. The desperate desire to please her.

Her heart turned over and warmth pooled low in her belly. She smoothed the pads of her fingers over his strong jaw and brushed a wave of black hair from his forehead.

"Just you, Dominic," she whispered. "I just want you."

His body heaved on a rough exhalation. He tasted her mouth before he lowered his dark head to her breasts. A whimper of pleasure left her when he parted her thighs and explored, testing her readiness. She succumbed and dropped her head back, curling her fingers in the soft waves of his hair, relishing the gentle sweeps of his tongue and the heat of his touch.

Her hands scrambled across his broad back when he rolled to the side, retrieving protection from the nightstand. He returned quickly, donning it, then teased the soft skin at the back of her knee and lifted her thigh over his hip, bringing them face-to-face.

Her eyelids fluttered shut when he kissed her fore-head and gently eased inside. His warm fingers moved into her hair and he touched his lips to hers. He tempered his movements, adjusting to each of her gasps and moans and reaching deeper. So deep, he stirred her soul.

Cissy gripped his muscular back, pleasure sweeping through her in a rush. Dominic swallowed her sigh with his mouth, his movements slowing as he was over-taken, too. Moments later, he drew her tighter to him and wrapped his hand in her hair.

Her body throbbed; her skin tingled. How she loved this man. She'd never felt so alive before. She'd never felt so at home. So cared for. So loved.

It wasn't until her heart slowed that she realized that although Dominic's body had shown the same, he'd never actually said it back.

Everything.

Dominic wound his fingers deeper in Cissy's hair and tucked her blond head under his chin. He shifted his hips, his heart tripping at her soft cry. The nagging thought that he should take care of things kept intruding but he couldn't make himself part from her yet.

Everything. That was what she'd given him. Three words. That was all it had taken to bring him to his knees.

He snatched in a ragged breath, still reeling. Her soft scent coated his skin, her sweet taste lingered on his tongue and her tender touch still pulsed inside his heart. He'd never felt so complete and at peace.

Or so afraid.

She moved as if to pull away and he smoothed his palm over the soft ivory skin of her back, keeping her against him. He opened his mouth to speak but it went dry, his tongue clinging to the back of his teeth.

It wasn't the words that held him back. It was what lay on the other side of them. The expectations. Responsibilities. The risk of failure. Failing her.

He gripped her slender frame tighter. He'd be damned if he'd do that.

A good man.

He winced. Those damn words had begun to haunt him. They taunted him, sending a shiver over his skin. He was just another man out here. He'd always known that. The only place he'd ever stood out was the arena. Where his talent and strength garnered respect and admiration. There, he was everyone's hero.

Out here, he was no one. Just another guy falling in the shadow of so many others. Nothing special.

But was that all there was? Was there no in-between? Did it have to be all or nothing?

He wasn't a saint by any stretch. Didn't even think he qualified as what Cissy termed a good man. But damned if he wasn't turning out to be a better man than he'd been. And he could be better still if it meant having Cissy and the boys to come home to.

His blood ran cold. *The boys.* Kayden and Jayden. There hadn't been a day since he met them that they hadn't looked up to him. Tugged at his hands. And his heart. What was it they saw in him? But, even worse, how the hell could he risk letting them down?

"Dominic?"

Cissy's voice prompted him to loosen his hard grip on her. She eased back to look up at him, her brow furrowed and cheeks flushed. Questions filled her eyes and hovered on the next breath she took. Questions that were too demanding. Ones he had no answers for.

"Come with me." He cupped her face, savoring the pink heat of her skin under the brush of his thumbs.

She blinked, glancing down at his chest before asking, "You're still leaving?"

He pressed closer, deeper. "I have to. But I want you with me. Come with me to the invitational." It was a start, at least. "To Atlanta."

Disappointment clouded her features. "But the boys—"

"Bring them. They've never been to a competition before, have they?"

A strand of blond hair slipped over her face as she shook her head. "No, they haven't. But it's a long drive from here. They didn't enjoy the trip the first time."

"I'll ask Logan and Pop to come." He brushed the hair from her face and placed a kiss on the tip of her nose. "It'll be a chance for us all to spend some time together. Let's just give it a try, Cissy."

She hesitated, running her tongue over her lips and looking away. "Okay." She looked back at him, expression wary. "We'll give it a try."

That was all he needed. One try. Once chance to show Cissy the better side of him. The man who wasn't afraid. The one who had no trouble grabbing a challenge and wrestling it to the ground. And, God help him, he hoped she saw that man. Because he didn't know how to be any other.

Chapter Ten

"It's so loud, Aunt Cissy," Jayden shouted.

A yank on her shirt prompted Cissy to stop midstride and look down. Jayden curled his fists into the hem of her T-shirt and shoved his head under it, burying his face in her waist and dislodging a handful of popcorn from the bucket in her hand.

Music boomed louder from the PA system and vibrated through the floor at their feet. Sporadic chatter and laughter burst around them, boisterous movement on all sides. The PBR event had hit high gear in Atlanta's Gwinnett Center.

"It's awesome," Kayden yelled over his shoulder, stamping his feet and throwing his arms over his head from several steps in front of them.

"Slow down, Kayden." Cissy maintained a firm grip on the bucket of popcorn in her hand and wiggled a cup of soda underneath her arm. She nudged Jayden's cowering form with her elbow. "Jayden, please. Just wait a minute until we sit down."

"But…lo…oud," he mumbled from underneath her shirt.

Cissy strained to make out his garbled response, stumbling over his feet and spilling another pile of popcorn. He rubbed his face against her belly and left a warm trail of slobber on her skin.

"I know it's loud, Jayden, but—"

"Aunt Cissy, there's a bull over there." Kayden jerked to a halt and shoved his face in between the heads of a couple sitting in the aisle below them. He pointed earnestly, his arm knocking the baseball cap off the man's head.

Cissy mouthed *I'm sorry* to the man and offered an apologetic smile. "Kayden, say excuse me and get back over here."

Kayden blinked back at her, eyebrows raised and jaw hanging open, then turned back to the couple, helping the man right his hat on his head. "'Scuze me." He tapped the man on the shoulder. "You see the bulls?" His voice rose with his excitement. "There's a bunch of 'em over there."

"They see the bulls, Kayden," Cissy gritted. "Now get back over here."

Kayden sprang back and rushed over to tap Jayden's head through the cover of her shirt.

"They got 'em out, Jayden." He bounced in place, grabbing a handful of the material and stretching it to peek at Jayden underneath. "The bulls, you know? The bulls!"

Kayden's excited jostling dislodged the lid to the cup, and a gush of cold soda flooded Cissy's armpit. The lights snapped off, plunging them into darkness. The crowd let out a collected whoop.

"They turned out the lights, Aunt Cissy." Kayden stated the obvious right before his hands clamped on to her arms, spilling more soda and popcorn.

Nice. Real nice. Now she could add being blind to

the physical handicap the boys had already given her. People lining the seats on both sides of them surged upward, dancing to the music and adding to the chaos. Something sticky on the floor clung to the bottom of her shoe, making it difficult to take a steady step.

Cissy counted to ten before groping around for Kayden's hand. Snagging it, she took a firm grip on it and lowered her head to shout, "You have to stick with me if we're going to make it to the seats. I need your help, okay?"

"Okay," Kayden yelled back.

"Here." She shoved the popcorn into his hand, feeling to make sure he held it with both hands. "You walk ahead of us but don't go too far. Follow the lights on the floor, okay?"

"Yes, ma'am," Kayden returned.

Cissy relocated the half-empty soda to her hand, then tugged Jayden's head out from under her shirt. "Come on, Jayden. There's not enough room for us to walk like this. You've got to get behind me and hold my hand. You can cover your ears back up when we sit down."

Thankfully, he complied. Cissy kept a firm grip on Jayden and grappled her way down the aisle behind Kayden. She kept track of his progress by trailing his shoes as they gleamed in the spotlights twirling about the stadium.

"Over here, Cissy."

Pop's deep call couldn't have been more welcome. Cissy barely made out his waving profile a few seats down. She reached out and bumped Kayden on the back with her wrist.

"There's Pop, see? Up on the left."

"I see—"

Heavy metal banged through the speakers, causing all three of them to jump. Flames flashed from the dirt floor of the arena, spilling flickers of light into the stands and escalating the crowd's cheers. A giant PBR emblem, on fire, glowed below them. Fireworks and strobe lighting exploded on either side, smoke billowing out among the sparks.

"You see that, Aunt Cissy?" Kayden stood mesmerized, his small form now highlighted in the glow of the pyrotechnics.

"Yeah," she said.

Cissy halted and attempted to get her bearings. An announcer blared on the PA system, introducing the riders. Each bull rider sauntered out in turn from the curtained entrance.

"Where's Mr. Dominic?" Jayden piped from behind, gripping her waistband.

"I don't know. He'll be out soon," she shouted back. "Let's get our seats so we can see him."

Cissy reached Kayden and gave him a nudge, then picked her way carefully down the remainder of the aisle. Soon they were standing in front of their seats beside Pop, the boys gazing at the spectacle below.

"Quite a sight, isn't it?" Pop yelled over the racket.

"Yeah." Cissy exaggerated her nod over the boys' heads, then faced the scene before them.

She swallowed hard and sifted through the men moving across the arena, straining for a glimpse of Dominic. It was exciting. She couldn't help but admit that. But Jayden had been right. It was also loud, fast and overwhelming. And, most disconcerting, it all seemed so distant. As if it were occurring in another place and time. Apart from the real world.

And she didn't even want to think about what could happen during a ride. Her nerves were shot as it was. She shuddered and sought comfort in attending to the boys.

Cissy wrapped her arm around Jayden's shoulders and leaned down to press a kiss to his cheek. "Are you okay now?"

Jayden looked up, smiling big and scooting forward in his seat. "Yep. I want to see Mr. Dominic."

Cissy sighed. So did she. And at the moment, he seemed a million miles beyond their reach.

The announcer continued to barrel out names and titles but paused several minutes later. "And in top position, grown here at home, current world champion, Dominic Slade."

The seat behind Cissy's legs almost lifted with the crowd's cheering surge.

"There he is," Kayden hollered, exchanging excited glances with Jayden.

Cissy followed the point of Kayden's finger to the back edge of the arena. Dominic emerged among the flashing strobe lights and puffs of smoke, striding to the center of the ring. A black vest and chaps hugged his muscular frame. With his black Stetson, he rose a head above the rest of the men, striking and formidable.

"That's Mr. Dominic, Pop," Jayden shouted, bouncing in the aisle.

Pop's proud countenance beamed even brighter. "I know, buddy."

Dominic stepped to the front of the line of cowboys, removed his hat and waved it to the crowd. The cheers grew louder. Stomping was added to the mix, rattling the stands under their feet. A chant began to chain around the stadium.

"Stomp and roll. Stomp and roll. Stomp and roll."

Cissy leaned over Kayden to call out to Pop, "What do they mean?"

"He always lands feetfirst." He cupped his hand around his mouth and leaned closer. "Rides till his eight are up then jumps off. Rolls outta the way."

"Every time?"

"Mostly." Pop frowned for a moment. "There's always those times, you know?" He turned and issued a comforting wink. "But he's careful. Respects the animal."

Cissy's stomach churned. Dominic had turned to the opposite side of the ring, whirling his hat over his head before placing it back and exiting with the other riders.

She inhaled deeply and fidgeted in her seat. The cup of soda in her hand dented beneath her tight clutch. Fat drops of cold condensation and soda streamed down her wrist, sending a shiver through her bones.

"Cissy." Pop's hand landed on her knee. "He's always careful. You can't expect more than that in this sport."

She nodded, managing a small smile. Sure. It was no secret the sport was dangerous. But it was one thing knowing it and another actually witnessing it. Cissy gnawed on the inside of her cheek. Especially, if you knew—and loved—the rider.

"Pop, when's Mr. Dominic's ride?" Kayden settled back in his seat and munched a mouthful of popcorn.

"Not for a while," Pop said. "Logan texted, said he was later in the lineup."

Well, that was a relief. At least she had some time to calm her nerves and prepare for the onslaught of tension ahead. Cissy eased back in her seat as well, straightening the straw on the drink with shaky fingers.

"Aunt Cissy?"

She stopped, the straw touching her mouth, and looked down at Jayden.

He scrunched up his face and whispered, "I gotta pee."

One hour, two bathroom trips and four hot dogs later, they all stared anxiously at the cowboys milling around the bull pens. Cissy tensed. Dominic was due up any minute.

She could just make out his profile as he straddled the bull, Chaos, in the chute below. As Dominic maneuvered into position, the announcer peppered the audience with tidbits on the bull's quirks. Unpredictable rolls, jaw-breaking kicks and four-foot leaps into the air were hallmarks of the burly, black-haired beast.

Cissy's heart hammered. Every ride up to this point had been a violent, bone-jarring spectacle. Each bull jumped higher than the one before and each rider slammed harder into the dirt. At times, it was gut-wrenching to watch.

"Mr. Dominic still has his cowboy hat on." Jayden frowned up at Pop. "Where's his helmet?"

"He's old school, buddy." Pop's gaze remained on Dominic. "Says he rides better without it." He shrugged. "Been that way since he was a kid."

"Bet he don't even need it," Kayden boasted, lifting his chin.

"They all need it," Cissy muttered. She tried to still the nervous bounce of her legs. "Only three have managed to make it so far. What are Dominic's odds?"

Pop sat up straighter, his chest lifting. "Real good."

Cissy's teeth began to chatter. "Do you think he'll stay on?" she asked.

"My boy doesn't just stay on, Cissy." His eyes remained on Dominic, the admiration in his voice unmistakable. "He's gonna make that bull dance."

The announcer blared in once more, drawing the crowd's attention to Dominic's chute. A few shifts and settling movements and Dominic tipped his head. The gate clanged open.

Chaos barreled out of the chute, hind legs thrusting into the air to fling Dominic back against his haunches only to yank him forward on the return. The bull's tail whipped in all directions. Chaos kicked his hooves, spraying up clumps of dirt. The bull jerked its head and snot slung from its nose.

The hellish assault continued, the two seconds that followed suspended and drawn out. Then something changed.

Dominic dipped to the side, leaning with the bull's bend, then rose up, his brawny arm stretching above him in a graceful arc. Chaos snapped back, dragging Dominic back down, but the momentum was met with accepted ease. The bull and Dominic still rose and fell with fury but the actions were fluid and in tandem.

The crowd roared louder with each buck of the bull. Cissy's muscles tightened to the point of pain. She forced her head to the side but was unable to tear her eyes from Dominic.

Time passed in moments. Moments of violent elegance she'd never expected to find played out on the dirt floor below them. Dominic's and the bull's strength were at their height, meeting somewhere in the middle in mutual respect and culminating in a savage ballet.

It was breathtaking and heroic. Overwhelming yet empowering.

A buzzer sounded, signaling the end of eight seconds. The fluid motions ceased. The relentless bucking returned. Dominic scrambled to unleash his hand from the rope.

Cissy jumped from her seat, her throat closing. "He can't get loose—"

"He'll get it." Pop was on his feet, too. His voice shook. "Just hold on."

Fractions of a second seemed like an eternity as Dominic finally managed to wrangle his hand free. Dominic bolted from the bull's back just as it heaved, slamming to his feet in a crouch and rolling off to the side.

Cissy relaxed, her body sagging. The boys' squeals raked across her fragile nerves.

"He did it!" Kayden grabbed on to Pop's legs and jumped in excitement. "Mr. Dominic did it."

Surprisingly, a laugh burst from Cissy's mouth and a smile stretched her cheeks. Dominic had indeed done it. He'd outshone every other rider. Stood taller than any other man.

Dominic jogged to the side rail as the bullfighters enticed Chaos out of the arena. The crowd thundered in approval and he waved his hat once again. Kayden and Jayden yanked on Cissy's legs, jostling her frame. Their excited shouts and praises merged with those of the crowd.

Cissy cheered with them, her chest swelling much the same way as Pop's had before. Her heart squeezed, fit to burst. It was all she could do to keep her legs still when Dominic turned to stride out of the arena. Her eyes clung to him, every muscle in her body straining to go with him. To follow.

A heavy weight settled over her. Cissy stopped shouting, her energy bottoming out. Was this what Crystal had felt with Jason? Had she watched him perform, fallen for him all over again and been so driven to stay at his side that she was ready to follow wherever he led?

Crystal had loved Jason. She'd declared it a thousand times over the years. And she'd never once hesitated to rush after him when he'd swept through town. There was no question—when Crystal had followed, she'd been happy with Jason.

But at what cost?

"Wasn't it great, Aunt Cissy?"

A tug on her shirttail focused Cissy's attention back on the boys. Jayden clutched one of her hands, Kayden the other. Smiles engulfed both their faces as they looked up at her. They bounced and chattered with excitement, contentment shining from their eyes.

Cissy froze. She knew exactly what price Crystal had paid.

DOMINIC SCRAWLED HIS signature across what seemed like the millionth T-shirt and shifted his weight to his other leg. The first round had ended, and he was on the ass end of an hour of fan meet and greets. He glanced up, scanning the stands but couldn't pinpoint Cissy or the boys among the scattering of attendees weaving their way to the exits.

He sighed. At least the crowd had dwindled down to a handful of people and the arena was almost empty again.

"Can I get a quick picture, Dom?"

Dominic glanced up, smarting at the sharp pain slashing through his neck, and nodded at the redhead waving a cell phone in front of her chest. Handing off the shirt to a fan, he propped his hands on his hips and assumed the preferred public relations stance.

"Fantastic," the redhead gushed.

The phone flashed and clicked, leading Dominic to relax. But she thrust the phone into her friend's hands and rushed over, pressing against his side and wrapping an arm around his waist. He smothered a wince as she bumped into his tender ribs.

She blinked up at him and grinned. "Just one more with me, okay?"

Dominic complied, disentangling her hands from him after the phone's next flash and easing away.

"Sorry, that's it." He tipped his hat and turned, his eyes scouring the stands once more.

Still no sign of Cissy or the boys. He rubbed a hand over his side, trying to smooth away the soreness. It'd been a good ride. One of his best, even. But damned if he couldn't wait to get off the dirt and back on solid ground with Cissy. He'd tried several times to snag a glimpse of her before and after his bout with Chaos but had been unsuccessful.

"If you're looking for someone, I think I found 'em."

Logan appeared at his side, grinning. He held Kayden and Jayden back with a finger in their belt loops. The boys cackled, straining against his hold and waving their arms and legs in circles in an effort to escape.

"That was awesome, Mr. Dominic." Kayden beamed up at him with both arms outstretched.

Dominic laughed, reaching down gingerly to slip his hands under the boy's armpits and haul him up to his chest. Kayden wrapped his legs tight around his waist and snuggled close. The soreness in Dominic's ribs increased to a painful throb.

"Just awesome," Kayden whispered again. He pecked a kiss against Dominic's cheek and planted his face in his neck.

Dominic smiled. Any pain he'd felt receded. That warm peace returned, filling his chest.

Jayden managed to escape Logan's hold and clutch Dominic's leg. "Yeah. It was great, Mr. Dominic."

"I'm glad y'all enjoyed it," he murmured, smoothing a hand over Jayden's blond head at his thigh.

"Careful, boys."

A gentle hand on his lower back accompanied Cissy's voice. Heat rushed through Dominic's body as she lifted Kayden away from his chest, her touch brushing over him.

"Mr. Dominic had a rough ride." She lowered Kayden to the ground then whispered in Dominic's ear, "How bad are you hurt?"

Dominic nuzzled her temple, then curled his hand around her nape. "I'm fine. Much better now, in fact."

She issued a broken smile, her lips barely moving.

"What did you think?" he asked, hating the uncertainty in his tone.

A real smile appeared, her face blushing. "It was—" she moved her hands as though trying to catch the words "—beautiful."

Beautiful. He didn't think anyone had ever used that word in reference to bull riding. But the way it rolled off her tongue had his toes curling in his boots.

"Almost perfection, son," Pop added.

Kayden skipped over to snag one of Pop's hands,

swinging it between them. "Yeah," Kayden quipped. "It was perfect."

Dominic grunted. "I wouldn't go that far." He rolled his shoulders. "I'm gonna have to soak for at least an hour tonight to get through the next round tomorrow."

Jayden's hands tightened around his leg, his head swiveling to the side. "Can't we stay for tomorrow, Aunt Cissy?"

Dominic tensed, his eyes shooting back to Cissy's. "You're leaving?"

She nodded, nibbling on her lower lip. "We need to get back. The boys may not look like it but they're worn out."

"So we'll take them to the hotel and put them to bed." His fingers massaged her neck with nervous motions. "They'll be good to go by morning."

"Yeah," Kayden added. "We'll be good to go by morning, Aunt Cissy."

Cissy shook her head, opening her mouth to speak but no sound emerged.

"Logan, why don't you and I take the boys outside and get some fresh air?" Pop wiggled his free hand at Jayden, who reluctantly released Dominic to amble over to him. Jerking his chin at Cissy as he passed, Pop added, "We'll get settled in the truck and be ready for whatever you decide."

"Thanks," she mumbled.

Dominic just caught the hard set of Logan's jaw before they all moved away, making their way toward the exit. The boys trailed behind Logan and Pop, Jayden craning his neck to keep sight of Dominic over his shoulder with a worried expression. Dominic's anxiety heightened and his hand tightened at the back of Cissy's neck.

"What's going on here, Cissy? I thought you knew this was a two-day event."

She nodded, gaze straying over his left shoulder. "I knew. I just… I need to get the boys settled."

"So we'll get them back and settled tomorrow," Dominic said. "After the last round."

"That's not what I mean," she whispered, eyeing the few stragglers milling about the arena.

"Look at me." He gripped her upper arms, tugging her closer to him. "I'm right here. Talk to me."

She looked at him then, those blue eyes of hers wary but determined. His gut knotted.

"Please understand," she said. "I need to get the boys settled. This trip with you was fun but—" she licked her lips "—we have to get settled."

"I'm still not following you." He dipped his head to peer at her. To try to make some sense out of what she was saying.

Cissy stiffened, drawing herself to her full height. "I mean this is good fun for a weekend every now and then, but that's all."

"Good fun for a weekend?" Even he winced at the bitterness in his tone. He drew his head back. "This is who I am, Cissy."

She bristled. "This isn't who you are. This is just something you do."

"Okay, I'll give you that. It's something I do. But it's important to me."

"I know it is, and I'm not trying to take that away from you—"

"Then, what are you trying to do?"

"I'm trying to get you to understand this won't turn out to be just a two-day event. It'll be one weekend before another, then another. Month after month. Just like you've spent all the ones before this summer. I can't plan my nephews' schedule around your trips," she blurted out. "They need to be settled. Somewhere permanent. Someplace that's home. This isn't the kind of life Kayden and Jayden can flourish in. And if it's not the right kind of life for them, then it's not the right kind of life for me."

That he understood. It hit its mark. A shot right to his chest. His hands dropped from her to hang at his sides.

"So you're giving me an ultimatum," he said. "That's what's really going on here."

Her face softened. "It wasn't intentional. I didn't come out here with this planned." She stepped forward, smoothing her hands over his vest. "The last thing I'd ever want to do is force you to choose between me and a career you love."

"But you're doing it anyway," he forced out. "You're making me choose."

He tried, without success, to suppress the sneer that crept over his face. He'd always known how fragile and fickle a woman's love was. And it always came at a price.

"You say you love me but threaten to leave," he continued. "Plan to walk away before we even really start. What the hell kind of love is that?"

Her face paled, her expression contorting with pain. Immediately, regret flooded him, closing his throat and burning his eyes. She drew back from him and wrung her hands in the hem of her shirt.

"I don't know," Cissy whispered. "I've never been

in love before. Maybe it's wrong but that's how I feel." She looked up then, studying him. "I'm being forced to choose, too. I have to choose between being with you or doing right by the boys. I love them just as much as I love you. And the last thing they need is another adult putting someone else before them." A breath shuddered from her. "My sister loved them but she did it all the time. Every time she took off with Jason she put her needs before theirs. I can't do that to them, Dominic. I won't."

His jaw clenched so tight, he thought his teeth would shatter. "And here's Jason again. The root of all your problems, right? Forgive me, Cissy, but he didn't come off as the devil incarnate when I met him."

Her eyes flashed. "I never said he was—"

"You made it plain all the same." Dominic balled his fists. *A good man*. He strained to hold back the words rising in his throat but he was desperate for reassurance. "Maybe I don't see myself as all that different from Jason. Maybe we're more alike than you think."

"Maybe you are," she said softly.

His heart stopped. Her response killed him. He had to inhale to reassure himself he was still alive.

"Right now, you're both on a stage," Cissy gestured to the empty stadium surrounding them. "The only difference is, instead of holding on to a mic, you're holding on to a bull."

Dominic swallowed hard, his ears ringing. "This is who I am," he rasped.

She shook her head, her eyes welling. "This is just a distraction. A distraction from the risks you're too afraid to take."

"You don't think I take a risk every time I climb on the back of a bull?"

"Yes, but that's a physical risk." She brushed a tear away, eyeing his frame. "We both know you can handle that. I'm talking about a bigger risk. One that hurts you on the inside." Her chest jerked on a silenced sob. "I hurt, too. It hurts to face this. But at least I'm willing to take a chance. At least I'm trying."

He couldn't speak. The three words he wanted to say lay trapped somewhere deep inside him, beyond his reach. Her hand wrapped around his forearm, her fingers trembling.

"I know what I'm up against. I know what you have here. But I love you more than any number of people that could fit into this place. So do the boys." She squeezed his arm. "You told me you wanted it all. That you wanted everything. So do I. That's probably not fair. I shouldn't expect it. Shouldn't even ask. But I guess, deep down, I was hoping I wouldn't have to ask. I was hoping you would offer to take a chance on me, too."

Dominic couldn't look at her. He was too empty. Too afraid.

All he could see was that she'd chosen to rank him low on her list of priorities. Chosen to walk away from him. And taken the boys with her. Because she didn't need him.

He hadn't measured up for Cissy. Hadn't measured up for Logan. Or his mom. Could never measure up.

Dominic shut his eyes to keep it all at bay. He refused to allow another bitter memory to take up residence beside the one he already carried. Silence descended, the air heavy between them. He tensed at the soft press of her mouth against his cheek.

"Goodbye, Dominic." Her voice broke, her hair brushing his face as she turned away.

Bye, Dominic. His cracked heart gaped into a chasm then crumbled to pieces.

He did look then. Forced his eyes open to watch her walk across the arena and slip out of sight. And cursed himself a thousand times over for a fool.

That was all he could be. A fool. Certainly not a good man. Not even just a man. Because if he were a man of any worth, the two women he loved wouldn't have been able to break his hold and leave him behind. And he wouldn't have let them.

No. He wasn't a man. Because what kind of man was too afraid to love?

Chapter Eleven

Rain pelted against the windshield and roof of the truck, drowning out Logan's commentary and, thankfully, Dominic's thoughts. The scene outside the passenger window blurred and smeared under the torrential downpour. Even in the early morning hours everything seemed enveloped in darkness. Dominic rubbed his hand over his forehead in an attempt to ease the throbbing headache he'd had since they'd left the Gwinnett Center.

The invitational had ended sooner than expected. He'd placed first and earned another check, which he'd promptly shoved in his back pocket. It'd only taken him a handful of minutes to gather up his gear, locate Logan and get the hell out. A restless night in a motel room had him rising before the crack of dawn and urging Logan back on the road.

Only, he'd forgotten how long the ride home would be. Without the boys. Without Cissy. And, at this point, was there really any reason to return anyway?

"...stop to get a bite?"

Dominic blinked, only catching the tail end of Logan's question. He looked away from the window and shook his head. "No. Just keep going."

His skin prickled as Logan's eyes bore into him before he turned his attention back to the interstate. The truck growled as it accelerated, the windshield wipers swiping with fury. A green sign emerged ahead.

Dominic straightened in his seat and gestured toward the ramp. "Take the next exit."

Logan narrowed his eyes on the sign then glanced at him in confusion. "That's not it. Our exit isn't for another fifty miles or so."

"Your exit," Dominic replied. "Mine is this one. Next event's about four hundred miles in the other direction. Colt always camps out at the motel off this ramp when he's on the circuit. I'll catch a ride with him."

Logan slowed the truck and turned to gape at him. "What the hell, Dom?"

"Just take the next exit."

"Pop's waiting for you at the ranch. Not to mention Cissy and—"

"Take the exit, Logan." The turn was almost on them. Dominic jerked forward, rapping his knuckles on the windshield. "You're gonna miss it."

Logan pounded his foot on the brake and jerked the truck to the shoulder of the road. Coins in the cup holder clanged as the truck bounced over uneven ground and jostled them about the cab. Dominic braced his hands on the dash just as the truck slammed to a stop.

"What the hell are you doing?" Dominic yelled.

"Get out," Logan spat.

"What?"

The cars speeding by wobbled the cab with strong rushes of wind. Each vehicle missed them by inches. Dominic cringed.

Logan thrust his door open and clambered out into

the rain. Horns blared and tires screeched as he made his way around the front of the truck to the passenger side. Dominic's door swung open with a wet, angry Logan heaving breaths on the other side.

"Get out of my truck."

Dominic's own fury rose, clawing at his gut and coating his words. "You're out of your damn mind," he muttered. "Get back in and let's go."

"Nope." Logan set his jaw, lifted it in the air then stabbed a finger into Dominic's chest. "You get your ass out. You want to go backward, you can damn well walk."

"I don't know what the hell you're talking about," Dominic gritted, settling back in his seat and ignoring the catch in his voice.

"Yeah, you do. I told you not to proceed if you didn't plan on following through." Logan words dripped with disdain. "I'm not helping you abandon Cissy and those boys."

Dominic sneered. "Here we go again with the preaching. Don't think you're the expert seeing as how you did such a fine job holding your own family together."

"We're not talking about me right now."

"Maybe we should."

Logan nodded. "Okay. Let's talk about me. And Pop, maybe? Let's talk about how we sat around for months on end hoping to catch a glimpse of you in person rather than on the TV."

Dominic shifted his attention back to the traffic whipping by. "That's bullshit, Logan."

"Nope. What's bullshit is you pulling the same trick you've pulled over and over for the past seven years."

Logan grabbed him with hard hands. "Now get your ass outta my truck."

Caught off guard, Dominic scrambled for a handhold as Logan yanked him toward the ground. His body, still recovering from the recent bout with the bull, balked with pain as he resisted Logan's efforts.

"Cut it out," Dominic shouted, rage sparking to life inside him.

"Hurts, doesn't it? Trying to hold on while someone's pulling in the opposite direction?" Logan heaved again, snatching him from the seat and onto the slippery grass. "You getting a taste of how Cissy feels yet?"

That spark of rage blasted into a burst of fire. It seared through his veins, burning his eyes and lungs. "How the hell would you know how she feels?"

Dominic thrust his fists into Logan's chest, his feet sliding over the slick ground. Scrambling for a grip on Logan, Dominic lost his footing and tumbled down the embankment, dragging Logan with him as he slammed into the ditch. Stunned, he lay on his back for a moment, drawing in deep gulps of air. Logan groaned at his side and rolled to face him.

"How do I know?" Logan mused, gasping and squinting his eyes against the rain. "Maybe because I feel the same way every time my little brother leaves without a backward glance at me."

Dominic exhaled, his anger fizzling out and remorse seeping in. The downpour slowed to a drizzle and the whoosh of cars passing on the highway rasped in his ears.

"Or maybe," Logan added, "it's because I've felt it every damn day since Amy left." He frowned against the drops hitting his face. "I'm not even entitled to that since I all but pushed her out the door. But damned if it don't hurt just as much. If I ever got another shot, I'd fight like hell to hold on and right my wrongs. Any sacrifice is better than constant regret." Logan licked the rain from his lips. "Is that what you want? You want to wake up every morning for God knows how long regretting you weren't man enough when it really counted?"

"Hell, no," Dominic rushed out. "But I'm not sure I'm the kind of man Cissy needs. She says I'm a good man but I don't feel it. I don't even know what that means anymore."

Logan sighed. "A man's just the sum of his choices, Dominic. It's the choices you make that define who you are. You chose to help Cissy and those boys when they were strangers. Went out of your way to see to their welfare. Supported them ever since. That's the man she came to know. The same man I know." Logan lifted up on his elbow, nudging his arm with a fist. "You're not just a good man, Dom. When you choose to be, you're one of the best."

A wave of warmth swept over Dominic. It heated his skin against the chill left behind by the rain and lifted the blanket of gloom smothering his heart. He was more than a good man. According to Logan, he was one of the best. A strong, honorable man. A man his brother was proud to know. The same man Cissy saw.

Dominic hesitated, swallowing hard before saying, "But she walked away anyway."

"No, she didn't. She took a stand. Did what she thought was best for those boys." Logan sat up. "What would you have rather she did? Chose to roam with you instead of staying with those boys? Leave them like mom left us?" He shook his head. "That's not who Cissy is. You know that. That's why you love her so much."

Well, damn. His brother made more sense than he'd like. Dominic sat up, too, dragging a hand over his face and cringing with shame at what a fool he'd been.

"You do love her?" Logan prompted at his silence.

Dominic jerked his hands from his face. "Hell, yes, I do. I love all of them."

Logan cast him a knowing look. "Are they yours?"

His side tingled. The same side Jayden had clung to the night he'd brought them to Raintree. The night he'd brought them home.

"Hell, yes." Dominic's fierce words burst from his lips. "All three of them are mine."

Logan's smile called for one of his own.

"Well, then, I guess you can get your hardheaded ass back in my truck." Logan grunted as he got up. "I'm getting too old for this shit."

"Old is right," Dominic lifted a brow with humor, rising and stretching his legs. He sobered then embraced Logan. "Wiser, too, as much as I hate to admit it," he added with a couple slaps to his brother's back. Drawing back, he asked, "Think you can use an assistant manager at Raintree? Maybe consider taking stock in bulls?"

"Taking up the reins with a vengeance, huh?" Logan laughed. "Long as you're there, baby brother, I'm game for anything." He steadied himself and brushed off his jeans. "Ready?"

Dominic's legs were already carrying him up the hill. They retraced their steps to the truck, the uneasiness in Dominic's gut having dissipated. There was no regret, no discomfort or unease. Just a deep sense of longing to hold Cissy and the boys. Feel that overwhelming sense of pride and put down roots. See how much they could grow together.

His blood warmed. *Grow.* Maybe even add to their family tree with another child. A baby girl with Cissy's big blue eyes. Eyes that would see only this man. A man that was unafraid to love. One who wouldn't hesitate to choose his family over anything else in life.

Gripping the truck door, Dominic hefted himself into the driver's seat. He drummed his fingers on the steering wheel as he waited for Logan, eager to get back on the road. Back to Cissy and the boys. He'd had no control over his mother leaving. That was her choice. A choice that had nothing to do with him or the family she'd left behind. But he didn't have to make the same one.

He no longer wanted or needed the approval of thousands. He only wanted and needed it from Cissy and the boys. To be the man he wanted to be, he only needed their love. And, most important, to love and support them the way they deserved.

His chest swelled. Without a doubt, choosing Cissy and the boys was already the best decision he'd ever made. He just hoped she'd choose to give him another chance.

Chapter Twelve

"Aunt Cissy?"

Cissy started, the pile of folded clothes slipping from her hands and onto the dresser. She swiped the back of her hand over her eyes and turned to find Kayden and Jayden hovering on the threshold of her room.

"You two about ready?" Her voice shook. She swallowed the lump in her throat and gathered the clothes back up. Tossing them in her overnight bag, she faced the boys with what she hoped was more composure. "It's about time to head out."

They blinked up at her, Kayden with a guarded expression and Jayden with a frown. Cissy sighed. She'd expected them to be confused. They'd left for the weekend rodeo only to return early and be instructed to pack up to leave permanently.

Pop had driven them back to Raintree the first night of the invitational. Cissy thought it best to give the boys one last day of fun at the ranch before leaving. But no more than that. It would just be harder to leave. And she was already having to force herself to go through the motions that would sever her ties with Dominic.

Her chin trembled. This was much harder than she'd expected. Her breaking point was much closer than she'd thought. She hid it by running her tongue over her lips and diverting her attention back to packing the bag.

"Are you sad?" Jayden asked.

Cissy straightened. "No." *Liar.* "I'm not sad. I'm just ready to get going is all."

Unconvinced, Jayden moved closer and tugged on her arms. He reached up on his toes and the warmth of his palms brushed over her cheeks.

"But you look sad," Jayden said. "Is it because we have to go? 'Cuz I don't want to."

"Me, neither." Kayden shoved his hands into his pockets and dug the toe of his shoe into the carpet. "Why can't we stay here?"

Cissy lowered her head, easing her hair in front of her face. How could she explain? There was no way to tell the truth without hurting them. And that was the last thing she'd do.

"Well, the car's fixed," she said. "And you two have to start back to school soon. So it's time to go and get settled. Pop helped me find a new job. He has a doctor friend a few hours away in Springfield that needs some office help. And I thought we could look for a new apartment together before I start working." She ruffled Jayden's hair, a real smile peeking out through the fog of pain smothering her. "You two could pick the one you like the most. We can afford a nicer one now. You can both have your own room."

Jayden looked thoughtful. Kayden was still unimpressed.

"And the apartments I've lined up for us to look at are near a college. They have classes that I think will jibe with my new work schedule." She summoned up a wider smile. "We'll all have a new school. New friends. It'll be exciting. A new beginning."

Kayden trudged over and picked at the sheets on the bed. "But can't we do that here?"

Cissy struggled to silence the voice pleading the same argument in her head. She stuffed the last of her clothes into the bag with more force than necessary. "We can't mooch off Pop forever, Kayden. Don't you want to get a place of our own?"

"Not if it means leaving here. We won't get to see Pop and Mr. Logan." Kayden scowled, punching a pillow. He shot her an accusing glare. "And what about Mr. Dominic?"

"What about him?" She yanked the zipper on the bag shut.

"We can't just leave him, Aunt Cissy."

"We're not leaving him—"

"Yes, we are—"

"We're not leaving him," she snapped. "He left us." The boys froze.

Cissy's stomach dropped. The comment had sprung from her mouth before she'd had a chance to stop it. She clenched her eyes shut and dropped her head.

"Mr. Dominic wouldn't do that." Kayden's voice held a note of defiance. Tears pooled in his eyes.

"I didn't mean it that way," she said softly, floundering for the right words. "Mr. Dominic cares about both of you very much. But you know he travels a lot. And he had to leave, too. The trip we went on with him wasn't a break for him. It was a starting point for a longer one. One that will last a long time."

The silence continued, the boys exchanging glances.

"So we won't see him anymore?" Kayden whispered.

Cissy's throat tightened. She lowered to her knees and drew them both close.

"I don't know," she said. Forcing herself to meet their eyes, she continued, "But you'll see me. Every day. And we'll be together. As long as we're together, that's all that matters. Right?"

Jayden nodded slowly, winding his arm around her neck and rubbing her nape with his fingers. Cissy brushed a blond curl back from Kayden's brow and tapped his chin.

"Right, Kayden?"

"You didn't go with him." Kayden sniffed, dragging the back of his hand over his eyes and studying her expression. "You didn't go. You stayed with us 'cuz we're a team."

Cissy couldn't answer. His wide eyes saw more than any child's should, and her self-control was fragile. She couldn't risk it.

Kayden threw his arms around her, nudging Jayden out of the way. His painful squeeze was a welcome comfort. It soothed the ache in her heart. She smiled and squeezed back.

"I'll help, Aunt Cissy." Kayden grabbed one handle on the bag, dragging it to the edge. "Come on, Jayden."

Jayden moved to join his brother but hesitated. Scooting close, he whispered against her ear, "He'll be back, Aunt Cissy."

She sighed as he pulled back and smoothed his fingers over her forehead.

"He'll be back," Jayden repeated before joining Kayden to pull the bag off the bed.

Cissy tucked her hair behind her ears with trembling fingers and watched the boys drag her overstuffed bag across the floor and out of the door. The pain was still there but it didn't throb like before.

She firmed her mouth. They'd make it through this. Together.

An hour later, Cissy slammed the trunk shut on the Toyota and nodded with satisfaction. It had taken longer than she'd expected to load up. They hadn't arrived with much but were leaving with almost more than their car could hold.

"I wish you'd change your mind," Pop said, waving to the boys through the back window. He spun to face her and pleaded once more. "Just a few more days, Cissy. Let Dominic come to his senses."

"No." She hugged him tight. "It's hard enough to go as it is. The longer we wait, the harder it'll be."

"He'll come around," he murmured in her ear. "I know he will. He loves you and those boys too much not to."

Cissy relished the soothing stroke of Pop's hand on her hair. "I'm sorry. I just can't. I won't force it. I have to let him go." She kissed his cheek before opening the car door. "I'll call you when we get settled. The boys would love it if you could come visit. So would I."

Pop nodded and smiled tightly. Cissy started the car and began to make her way down the long dirt drive. She watched Pop in the rearview mirror as he stood waving. The only sound in the car was the flick of Kayden's rope against the back of her seat. Cissy managed to blink back the tears by the time they reached the highway.

They'd only made it a few miles before Jayden said, "I gotta pee, Aunt Cissy."

"And I'm hungry," Kayden added, smacking the rope against the seat once more.

Cissy smiled and shook her head. It was fitting that they have one last goodbye. "I know just the place."

The Peachy Keen Diner was standing exactly where they'd left it. The menus were just as colorful as ever and the tables just as greasy. Meat sizzled in frying pans and the busy clang of metal utensils sounded from the kitchen. It was very much the way it had been on their last visit.

Only, the group of morning patrons was a lot different from the one they'd mingled with the night they'd first entered. A few couples sipped coffee together and a set of grandparents beamed at small children over plates of breakfast. And there was a noticeable gap in the row of candy machines lining the wall.

Cissy pinched her lips to conceal her smile.

The boys headed straight to the restroom with Kayden's rope trailing behind them. Cissy placed an order for three burgers to go, then took up residence by the bathroom door.

Her lips twitched as she eyed the aged wood. The sign was still there. Still tattered as ever, an added scratch slashing through the *M* in MEN. She was surprised to find it still clinging to the door. She ran the tip of her finger over it and pressed the corner of the sign firmly in an effort to make it stick.

Tears welled over onto her lashes. She blinked them back, pressing her finger harder to the door. Funny how a silly, stupid sign could make her blubber. Fat lot of good it would do to cry over a beat-up sign. Or a beat-up heart.

"Need a little help, ma'am?"

Cissy stilled. There was no mistaking the deep tenor of Dominic's voice. It settled over her like a warm blanket, making her yearn to grab on and pull it close. Pull him close. Instead, she maintained her stance, scared to move in case he disappeared again.

Her mouth dry, she said, "I might. Why do you ask?"

Footsteps fell close behind her and his husky words made her ears tingle.

"Well, you look a bit confused." His large hand covered hers, obscuring the sign. "This is the men's room, you see?"

His thumb caressed the back of her hand. A delicious shot of pleasure overtook her, and she slipped from under his touch and turned, letting her eyes drink him in.

His black hair was tousled. His dark eyes bright. They peered down at her, his strong jaw tightening as he brushed away a tear hovering on her lashes.

"I was hoping the boys would need a pit stop," he murmured. "I was already having a hard time catching up."

Heat bloomed in Cissy's face. There was no stopping the tears now. They slipped from her lashes and tickled her cheeks.

"I thought you'd be on your way to the next event by now."

Dominic smiled, white teeth and dimples appearing. "I am. I had a much bigger event I needed to make it to."

"I don't understand—"

"This one." His finger drifted over her bottom lip, sending a wave of warmth to her belly. "The one where I make you an offer."

Cissy waited, air sticking in her lungs.

"An offer to take a chance on us," he continued. "A chance to love. To be a family."

Her heart floated but she shuffled her feet, keeping them firmly on the ground. "Dominic, there's nothing I want more. But I know you feel as if you have to do this, and I don't want you to give up something you love and then regret it later. I don't want you to resent—"

"The only regret I have is not manning up and telling you how I feel when you needed to hear it. And the only thing I resent is not choosing to do this sooner." He cupped her face with his big hands. "I love you. I love Kayden and Jayden. I choose you. All three of you. I want to marry you. Be a dad to those boys. And I want to give you everything. Give us everything."

"But you love bull riding. It's important to y—"

"I love you and the boys more," he stated firmly. A laugh burst from his lips. "And I have a feeling the three of you are gonna give me a more exciting ride than any bull ever could."

Cissy held on to his wrists, squeezing hard. It was almost impossible to believe the moment was real. She'd never expected...

She had to know he was sure. "I don't want to tie you down—"

"I want to be tied down, Cissy." He drew closer with a soft smile. Cissy's stomach flipped at his eager grin. "Hell, if I'm being honest, I'm more concerned with making sure I have you tied down."

Feet shuffled from behind. "Need my rope?"

Kayden's hand thrust between them, a smile wreathing his face and his frayed rope dangling in the air.

Dominic laughed and squeezed Kayden's shoulder. "Nah, that's okay, Kayden."

Jayden slammed the bathroom door, then shoved past Kayden to wrap his arms around Dominic's leg. He tipped his head back to beam up at Dominic. "I knew you'd come back."

Cissy released a pent-up breath when Dominic lowered to his haunches. He hugged the boys close, murmuring phrases of affection and kissing the tops of their heads. Looking up at her, he hesitated, asking, "So what do you think?"

Smiling at his boyish expression, she nodded and whispered, "Yes."

Dominic rose and pulled her against him. Face creasing with pleasure and devilry, he reached down and tucked the boys' faces against his legs, then kissed her. Deeply and soundly. Cissy sighed, her knees growing weak, and leaned into him.

"Let's go home," Dominic murmured against her mouth. Sweeping her up in his arms, he laughed deeper at her squeal. He glanced down and jerked his chin. "Boys, grab a leg. We're heading home."

"Back to the ranch?" Jayden's voice burst with excitement as he wrapped himself around one of Dominic's legs and held on tight.

"Yep."

Kayden climbed onto the other leg, asking with a grin, "To stay?"

"Yep."

Kayden jabbed her bottom. "Aunt Cissy, we're going back to the ranch."

Cissy jumped, batting Kayden's hand away and pushing at Dominic's broad chest with a laugh. "Dominic, let me down. We're too heavy. You can't carry all of us."

"Who says?" His sexy tenor rumbled beneath her

palm. Dropping a kiss on the tip of her nose, he hefted one muscular leg forward, then another, making his way across the diner. "I got this."

The boys squealed with delight and Cissy laughed when they drew to a halt at the exit.

Dominic shot her a rueful smile, dimples denting. "Might need some help with the door, though."

Cissy kissed his strong jaw and said, "We can manage it. Together." She tapped the blond heads beneath her and directed, "Boys, help us out here."

A good shove with her feet and their little hands swept the door open. Dominic carried them all through it. She kissed him again, savoring his soft moan of pleasure and the giggles drifting up from the boys.

Cissy held on tighter and smiled. They had more than she'd ever expected. They had everything.

* * * * *

Watching his young wife walk away almost destroyed Logan Slade. Now he's determined to get her back. But is he too late?

Don't miss THE RANCHER'S WIFE, April Arrington's next MEN OF RAINTREE RANCH novel.

Available August 2016.

REQUEST YOUR FREE BOOKS!
2 FREE NOVELS PLUS 2 FREE GIFTS!

HARLEQUIN®

American Romance®

LOVE, HOME & HAPPINESS

YES! Please send me 2 FREE Harlequin® American Romance® novels and my 2 FREE gifts (gifts are worth about $10). After receiving them, if I don't wish to receive any more books, I can return the shipping statement marked "cancel." If I don't cancel, I will receive 4 brand-new novels every month and be billed just $4.74 per book in the U.S. or $5.49 per book in Canada. That's a savings of at least 12% off the cover price! It's quite a bargain! Shipping and handling is just 50¢ per book in the U.S. and 75¢ per book in Canada.* I understand that accepting the 2 free books and gifts places me under no obligation to buy anything. I can always return a shipment and cancel at any time. Even if I never buy another book, the two free books and gifts are mine to keep forever.

154/354 HDN GHZZ

Name	(PLEASE PRINT)
Address	Apt. #
City	State/Prov.	Zip/Postal Code

Signature (if under 18, a parent or guardian must sign)

Mail to the **Reader Service:**
IN U.S.A.: P.O. Box 1867, Buffalo, NY 14240-1867
IN CANADA: P.O. Box 609, Fort Erie, Ontario L2A 5X3

Want to try two free books from another line?
Call 1-800-873-8635 or visit www.ReaderService.com.

* Terms and prices subject to change without notice. Prices do not include applicable taxes. Sales tax applicable in N.Y. Canadian residents will be charged applicable taxes. Offer not valid in Quebec. This offer is limited to one order per household. Not valid for current subscribers to Harlequin American Romance books. All orders subject to credit approval. Credit or debit balances in a customer's account(s) may be offset by any other outstanding balance owed by or to the customer. Please allow 4 to 6 weeks for delivery. Offer available while quantities last.

Your Privacy—The Reader Service is committed to protecting your privacy. Our Privacy Policy is available online at www.ReaderService.com or upon request from the Reader Service.

We make a portion of our mailing list available to reputable third parties that offer products we believe may interest you. If you prefer that we not exchange your name with third parties, or if you wish to clarify or modify your communication preferences, please visit us at www.ReaderService.com/consumerschoice or write to us at Reader Service Preference Service, P.O. Box 9062, Buffalo, NY 14240-9062. Include your complete name and address.

HARI5

"What are you doing here on your day off?" he asked.
"It's Sunday. The day of rest."

"Yeah, well, no rest for the wicked."

He let his voice drop and his eyes rove her face. "You're
not wicked, Vi." Though she could be flirtatious and fun
when she let loose.

For the briefest of seconds, she went still. Then—
strange for her, as Violet usually oozed confidence—she
turned away. "I asked you not to call me that."

"I like Vi. It suits you."

And it was personal. Something just the two of them
shared. Calling her Vi was his way of reminding her
about the night they'd spent together, which he supposed
explained her displeasure. She didn't like being reminded.

She'd made the mistake of telling him that Vi was a
childhood nickname, one she'd insisted on leaving behind
upon entering her teens. They'd been alone, lying in bed
and revealing their innermost feelings. Unfortunately, the
shared intimacy hadn't lasted, disappearing with the first
rays of morning sunlight.

"I was wondering. If you weren't busy later…" She let the sentence drop.

"I'm not busy." Cole leaned closer, suddenly eager. "What do you have in mind?"

Could she have had a change of heart? They weren't supposed to see each other again socially or bring up their one moment of weakness. According to Vi, it had been a mistake. A rash action resulting from two shots of tequila each, a crowded dance floor and both of them weary of constantly fighting their personal demons.

Cole didn't necessarily agree. Sure, the road was not without obstacles. As one of the ranch owners, he was her boss. On the other hand, *she* oversaw *his* work while he learned the ropes. Confusing and awkward and a reason not to date.

But incredible lovemaking and easy conversation didn't happen between just any two people. He and Vi had something special, and he'd have liked to see where it went, obstacles be damned.

Strange, he hadn't given her a second thought before their "mistake." One moment on a dance floor and, boom, everything had changed. A shame she didn't feel the same.

Unless she did and was better at hiding it? The possibility warranted consideration.

"We need to, um, talk." She closed her eyes and pressed a hand to her belly.

Don't miss
HAVING THE RANCHER'S BABY
by Cathy McDavid, available June 2016
wherever Harlequin® American Romance®
books and ebooks are sold.

www.Harlequin.com

Copyright © 2016 by Cathy McDavid

Same great stories, new name!

In July 2016,
the HARLEQUIN®
AMERICAN ROMANCE® series
will become
the HARLEQUIN®
WESTERN ROMANCE series.

Connect with us to find your next great read,
special offers and more.

f /HarlequinBooks

🐦 @HarlequinBooks

www.HarlequinBlog.com

www.Harlequin.com/Newsletters

❖ HARLEQUIN®

A *Romance* FOR EVERY MOOD™

www.Harlequin.com

Copper Ridge, Oregon's favorite bachelor is about to meet his match in this sweet and sexy story by *USA TODAY* bestselling author

MAISEY YATES

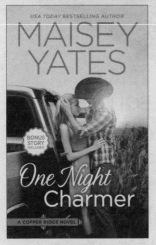

If the devil wore flannel, he'd look like Ace Thompson. He's gruff. Opinionated. Infernally hot. The last person that Sierra West wants to ask for a bartending job—not that she has a choice. Ever since discovering that her "perfect" family is built on a lie, Sierra has been determined to make it on her own. Resisting her new boss should be easy when they're always bickering. Until one night, the squabbling stops…and something far more dangerous takes over.

Ace has a personal policy against messing around with staff—or with spoiled rich girls. But there's a steel backbone beneath Sierra's silver-spoon upbringing. She's tougher than he thought, and so much more tempting. Enough to make him want to break all his rules, even if it means risking his heart…

Available now!

Be sure to connect with us at:

Harlequin.com/Newsletters
Facebook.com/HarlequinBooks
Twitter.com/HQNBooks